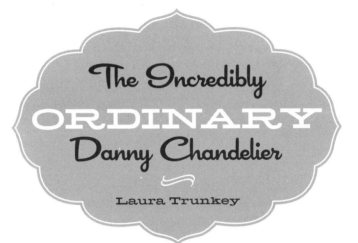

The Incredibly
ORDINARY
Danny Chandelier

Laura Trunkey

annick press
toronto + new york + vancouver

Edited by Pam Robertson
Copy edited by Tanya Trafford
Proofread by Kathy Evans
Cover design by Black Eye Design/Michel Vrana
Cover illustration by Niki Daly

We acknowledge the support of the Canada Council for the Arts, the Ontario Arts
Council, and the Government of Canada through the Book Publishing Industry
Development Program (BPIDP) for our publishing activities.

 ONTARIO ARTS COUNCIL
CONSEIL DES ARTS DE L'ONTARIO

Cataloguing in Publication
Trunkey, Laura
    The incredibly ordinary Danny Chandelier / Laura Trunkey.

ISBN 978-1-55451-139-6 (bound).—ISBN 978-1-55451-138-9 (pbk.)

    I. Title.
PS8639.R85I53 2008   jC813'.6   C2008-901584-3

Printed and bound in Canada

Published in the U.S.A. by	Distributed in Canada by	Distributed in the U.S.A. by
Annick Press (U.S.) Ltd.	Firefly Books Ltd.	Firefly Books (U.S.) Inc.
	66 Leek Crescent	P.O. Box 1338
	Richmond Hill, ON	Ellicott Station
	L4B 1H1	Buffalo, NY 14205

Visit our website at **www.annickpress.com**

For my mother, Marnie McKay,
who sees the extraordinary in everyone

Lily Brook Academy

Dear Future Lily Brook Resident,

Your family has made an exciting choice for your future. They realize how hard it is for you to feel like you don't belong, to know you'll never follow in their footsteps or live up to their expectations. They understand your longing to be with others who are like you: those with modest abilities, meager talents, and average intellect. These are the people you will encounter at Lily Brook Academy—ordinary people who were born into extraordinary families, just as you were.

At Lily Brook you will experience a sense of accomplishment that was never possible in schools dominated by your more intelligent peers. Classes are small and instruction is unsurpassed. We consider it our responsibility to ensure that every student achieves some amount of success, no matter how small. At Lily Brook your natural gifts and abilities will no longer be dwarfed by the genius of those around you, and being not so good will finally be good enough.

Some of our newcomers believe their families are ashamed of them, and that is why they are being sent to this facility at the base of Mount Poplova. This is far from the truth. Your family loves you and wants what is best for you. They, and we, are certain that what is best for you is Lily Brook, the next step on the path to the rest of your life. Welcome to Lily Brook. The adventure starts here.

Gladys and Richard Brook
Founders

I

AT THE AIRPORT, Mother sits perched on my mono-grammed trunk and lets the moving sidewalk wind us past the departure gates. She has my left hand trapped in both of hers and is squeezing so hard my fingertips have turned purple. The plane to Poplovastan leaves from Gate 13 at 2:00—which means there is one hour left for me to cross my toes and wish for a miracle.

I'm not hopeful.

I could cross my toes so hard they'd go numb. I could cross my legs, and arms, and eyes. But chances are good that in one hour and fifteen minutes I will be 40,000 feet above the earth, regardless. I'll be heading towards Lily Brook Academy, the piggy-faced couple on the brochure

I ripped into confetti and flushed down the toilet, and the "next step on the path to the rest of my life." My breakfast is threatening to splatter on my brand-new shoes.

We pass Gates 7, 8, and 9. Two girls in matching sundresses shriek and race across the rows of chairs, while a man with dark, wavy hair lunges for them. He grabs the smallest and sputters a raspberry against the side of her face. It feels like the lump that's been lodged in my throat for the past week and a half has dropped to my stomach and split into a dozen fluttering pieces. With my free hand, I wipe the wet blur of tears from my eyes. Soon Mother will be in the car, heading home without me.

Even though it's the middle of an August heat wave, Mother is wearing her ratty coat. She lets go of my hand to wrap it even more tightly around her, then dabs the beads of sweat off her forehead with her silk scarf.

We pass Gates 10, 11, and 12. A man and his son—a boy my age—are sitting cross-legged on the carpet near the ticket counter, each holding a fan of playing cards. As I watch them, the flutters tickling my rib cage spiral down the length of my body. My legs are like jelly, my kneecaps are tingling, and I can barely feel my feet. I try to focus on the patch of floor in front of me, but my eyes jump from one thing to the next: the wrinkles in the dress pants Mother bought me for the trip, the gumball in my mouth, which has dried out completely (along with my tongue), the other kids nearby—who all seem much too happy to be headed where I am. Mother rubs her cheek against the ragged fur collar of her coat. She is humming to herself.

We pass … Gate 14.

No Gate 13? Mother frowns, pulls out the Lily Brook Academy acceptance letter and studies it. She glances at the gate we've just passed, then turns and peers ahead.

No Gate 13!

I am ready to leap off the sidewalk and run back the way we came, down the hall, out the spinning glass doors, and into the parking lot. I am ready to wake Father's chauffeur and tell him to step on it, all the way back to Currency.

But Mother keeps her grip on my hand and shakes her head.

"Still farther, Danny." She puts the paper back into her pocket and wipes her nose with her sleeve.

And it is farther. Much farther. We ride the sidewalk until Gate 82, where the strip of rubber that's been carrying us all this way is sucked into a bump on the floor, and we are spit onto cement. Beside us a row of windows frame the tarmac, and one cargo plane after the next glints from below. I yank my trunk behind me and follow the green chalk arrows on the floor. The windows we pass become smaller and smaller, and the walls around us get tighter and tighter, until we are walking through a dim tube. Flickering light bulbs dangle from the ceiling, and the air conditioning is cranked so high that bursts of clouds leave my mouth when I breathe. At the end of the hall is a steel door with the word "RESTRICTED" stenciled on it in thick red letters. And on that door, just below the handle, there is a small paper sign: "Gate 13," it announces in a barely legible scrawl, "This Way, Lily Brook Residents."

Mother drops my hand and pulls the belt of her coat still tighter. She sniffs loudly and wipes her eyes on one of the matted fur cuffs. Her cheeks are streaked with eye makeup, and her face is puffy and red. She takes a gulp of air, then gives me a twitch of a smile that quickly shrivels to nothing. She nods her head, and I grab the handle, close my eyes, and pull.

IN THE TWO MONTHS that followed my grade six graduation from junior preparatory school, three things happened.

1. I failed the Midas Millions Academy entrance examination.

2. I failed a second time.

3. I failed the exam on my "third and final try."

Maybe it's not fair to blame everything on that one test. There are plenty of other things I've failed at in my life—lists and lists of them. But the entrance exam was, as my father put it, "the straw that choked the camel." It is the reason I am here, and not at home enjoying the last days of summer vacation with Archduke Pooch.

I suppose for things to make sense I should start even before grade six. I should start with my family and with my hometown. I should start by saying that when you grow up in a family of the rich and powerful, the brainy and beautiful, the practically perfect, being average is like being mud.

And I *am* average. I am average height and average weight with average-looking brown eyes and hair that is exceptional only because of the cowlick that won't lie flat unless my mother presses it down with spit. I am an average student who is sort of good at everything and great at nothing. Last year I got eighth place in the school spelling bee and tenth place in the science fair. I made the band, but the only instrument left was the triangle and I never got to hit it more than three times in any song. I survived the tryouts for four sports teams—but only as an alternate. And although my mother watched every football, baseball, basketball, and archery tournament at my school, she never saw me do anything but heat the bench with my rear end and lend out my equipment when the other players broke theirs. On my report cards my teachers always write: "Danny is a fine student" or "Danny is a fine young man."

My father says "fine" means forgettable.

Everything about me, Danny Chandelier, is average, but there is nothing average about the rest of the Chandelier family and there is nothing average about Currency, the place we're from.

Currency is what people call a gated community. Not because there are actual gates—there used to be, but my father had them ripped down and replaced by an electronic force field that he controls by remote from his office. He removed the real gates because it was the only way he could get my mother to marry him. She told him that her idea of happily ever after wasn't to marry the prince and move to a prison, and she wouldn't go near Currency until every last piece of stone and metal from the walls had been carted away. But, still, it's up to Father who can come in. And who has to leave.

Even though Currency has its own hill, lake, and forest and is double the area of Midasville—where my sisters and I go to school—it isn't a real town. That's because the actual population is just six and a half. I say half because my dog, Archduke Pooch II, is as smart as any person I know, but can't really be considered one. The other people who live in Currency are my mother and father, my three sisters, and me.

At least I used to.

II

BEHIND THAT DOOR marked Gate 13 is a room unlike any airport waiting room I've ever seen. The floor is concrete; studs and wiring stick out from an unfinished section of wall; and half the fluorescent lights that line the ceiling are broken. Instead of a check-in counter, there is a small wooden podium at the far end of the room. Instead of cheerful-faced airline staff, there are two scowling women in gray uniforms hovering near the doorway. And instead of plush seats to stretch out on, there are rows of uncomfortable-looking blue plastic chairs.

The room is already full of kids, probably close to thirty of them. Some are with one or both parents, and some are with women in white collared shirts and black skirts, like the outfit Father makes Isabella, our maid, wear. But most of them are by themselves. There are boys and girls, skinny kids and chunky kids, lanky kids and shrimpy kids, kids with every sneaker size and skin color imaginable. The only thing they seem to have in common, really, is that they all look miserable.

They look just about as miserable as I feel.

Mother and I sit on the pair of chairs closest to the exit. Beside us, a man and his son are hissing at each other in Spanish. A leather jacket is draped over the back of the man's chair, and the sleeves of his white button-down shirt are rolled up to expose muscular forearms. His hiking boots are scuffed and his hair windswept, as though he had emerged from the wilderness just to make an appearance here. He looks vaguely familiar, and perhaps others in the room think so as well, because most of the women are staring in his direction.

After a moment I recognize him. When Father goes on business trips to the stock exchanges, or to the various foreign banks he has accounts with, he brings hotel brochures home for Annabelle, because she wants to be a famous model someday and is already planning the destinations for her first round-the-world runway show. This man has smiled out from the inside cover of a half-dozen adventure-resort brochures, always pictured with his wife and two young, rosy-cheeked daughters. There's never been a son in any of the photographs—but even though the resemblance is slight I can tell that the boy with him is his son. They have the same full lips and broad nose, features that on the man seem exotic, but which make his son—with his round cheeks and eyes that are magnified by the lenses of his glasses—look oddly proportioned and bug-like. The boy is dressed similarly to his father in a leather bomber jacket, slim-cut jeans, a button-down shirt, and a pair of hiking boots, but instead of looking windswept, his hair is gelled into short spikes. And while his father's boots are scuffed and worn, the boy's look like they've never walked along a mountain trail. They're so shiny I can see my reflection in them.

The man has his hands around his son's wrists, but the boy yanks them away and screams something at him—so loudly that the rest of the conversations in the room come to a halt as the shout echoes once, and then again, off the cement walls.

"José!" the man barks, the word exploding like a fire-cracker in the quiet. Slowly he shifts in his seat and glances over his shoulder, at the other parents shaking their heads, at the trembling girls and sullen-faced boys—each of them staring in his direction. His hand shoots up to hide his face from sight as he grabs his jacket and rushes towards the door.

José slumps in his seat and thumps his heels against the chair legs. His cheeks and ears have turned deep crimson and, in his lap, he clenches his hands into fists. I feel bad for him, but when I turn to say hello he narrows his eyes into slits and twists so quickly in his seat that I end up introducing myself to his back.

Some of the other parents begin to file out through

the door, too, but Mother stays beside me. She is crying, and every so often raises our held hands to her face and rubs her cheek on my shirtsleeve. Before long my cuff is practically drenched.

She kisses my forehead. "Danny Boy," she starts, but at that same moment, Mr. Remroddinger, the little twitchy-faced man who I last saw slinking down our front path to his car, arrives at the podium at the front of the room. He is dressed in the same gray suit he was wearing that evening and carries the same small leather briefcase, which he places in front of him.

"Parents," he calls, snapping his fingers over his head. "Parents and various household staff. Your presence is no longer required here. It is time to say a last good-bye to your children, to send them forward on their journey as the future scholars and citizens of Lily Brook."

A couple of kids near me start to cry, and one girl grips her father's arm so tightly that he has to stand and shake her off, letting her tumble like a sack of onions onto the floor. As she reaches for him again, he steps over her, brushes imaginary dirt from his suit, and then passes through the exit beside me. More adults follow him, but still Mother sits and clutches my hand. Pressed against her, I can feel her body shaking.

"You, Ma'am." Mr. Remroddinger has one thin finger pointed at Mother. "Mrs. Chandelier, Mrs. Walkerton Chandelier. You may leave now, Ma'am."

Mother doesn't move, but holds my hand even tighter. Mr. Remroddinger snaps his fingers and motions towards

Mother and instantly the two uniformed women arrive at her side. Their stiff shirtsleeves are rolled past their elbows, and their heavy pants end inches above their ankles to show off the rows of silver buckles on their black leather boots. They each grab hold of one of Mother's arms and hoist her from her chair.

"Please," Mother cries, wrenching her arm free to smooth down the back of her coat. She lets her hand fall to the top of my head before she is led away. "I love you, Danny Boy," she wails. "Your mother loves you."

MAYBE MY MOTHER DIDN'T WANT to send me to Poplovastan, maybe she will miss me, but it sure seemed like she was the only one in the family who had a hard time saying good-bye.

Mother arranged for us to travel to the airport by limousine, an eight-hour drive. Father said the whole idea was ridiculous, that I was old enough to travel alone and, anyway, hadn't Mother ever listened when he explained that time was money? But Mother put her foot down and said that she wanted to be with me during my last hours in the country, and was that too much to ask, considering what he was making her give up? It wasn't a question, I suppose, because when Father tried to answer she grabbed her coat and left the room.

She told me I could invite my sisters along, but I wanted to be alone with her. Besides, I doubted they'd be able to pull themselves away from their important lives. Instead they lined up in the doorway this morning to see me off. Isabella was beside them on her hands and knees, scouring the grooves between the floor tiles with a toothbrush.

"Good-bye, Isabella," I said. She looked up, wiped the sweat from her face with the back of her hand, and grunted something before she continued scrubbing. Caroline—her swim goggles around her neck and a rugby ball tucked into the crook of her arm—touched my shoulder.

My father says that before my sisters and I were born, "the big guy upstairs" dished out the Chandelier gifts between us. Between them, that is. Maybe "the big guy" didn't realize my parents had wanted four children. It seems to me that he used up all the talents on my three sisters and didn't have much of anything left when I came along.

Caroline is the one who got all of the Chandelier athletic ability. She was walking at six months and by the third grade had made the school relay team. Her dream is to be the first female athlete to compete in every sport in the Olympics, and she spends most of her time practicing her "routine." This morning, as I packed my last few treasures into my trunk, I watched through my window as she pole-vaulted past the snow machines to the ski hill, luged down to the grassy field beside the velodrome, then zipped between the basketball court and the Perma-Frost Ice Rink (patent pending) that Father enlisted a team of chemical engineers to design for her birthday last year.

"There's a trail at the base of Mount Poplova, suitable for mountain biking, and a lake beside Lily Brook where one can swim, sail, and water-ski," she reminded me, quoting a caption from page five of the brochure. When she pulled me towards her and kissed my forehead, she smelled faintly of chlorine and sweat.

Brittany, my middle sister, tapped my arm with a test tube. Brittany has almost all of the Chandelier brains. She wants to be a scientist and spends every minute pouring chemicals into tubes and examining things under microscopes. Father says Brittany is on the brink of a number of startling scientific discoveries, and every so often he invites reporters around to see what she's working on. On her fifteenth birthday, he purchased the entire contents of the chemistry laboratory at her dream university and had a science warehouse built beside the pool.

"At Lily Brook Academy, the education is first-rate, with state-of-the-art facilities and instruction from some of the most learned minds in science and the humanities," Brittany quoted from page three. She pulled me into a hug, and then turned to Annabelle, my oldest sister. Annabelle was examining her face in the mirror beside Father's hat rack. She rubbed her cheeks until they were rosy, then sucked them in slightly so her lips pouted out. She turned sideways quickly and watched how the back of her skirt curled out around her knees. Brittany jabbed Annabelle with the test tube.

"Ouch!" Annabelle turned to glare at her. Out of the corner of my eye I saw Brittany point at me, and then mime a wave.

"Oh, right. Danny." Annabelle glanced one last time at the mirror before bending to give me a hug. "You'll have a, umm, a splendid time, I'm certain. And what a relief to know that a place like Lily Brook exists. It really is the best choice for a family member like you."

Father took my hand and shook it. "Decipher some Egyptian runes, Danny. Or find the cure for night blindness. Learn to wrestle crocodiles, or climb a mountain blindfolded. Make me proud."

III

WHEN THE TWO LARGE WOMEN return from hauling Mother away, one pushes a deadbolt across the door. They both stand inches in front of the exit, glaring at us with their arms crossed against their chests, legs apart, knees bent—clearly ready to wrestle the first person who tries to escape.

I shudder, and focus on the floor behind them, on the small crack between the steel door and the cement through which I hope to hear Mother calling out to me.

Nothing.

I feel around in my pocket until my fingers slide against the cool of the gold button tucked inside. I trace the ridges and grooves in the metal with my thumb, then pull it out and hold it against my cheek.

"Very well, then." Mr. Remroddinger clicks open his briefcase. "Now let's get started."

I close my eyes and think back to my ride to the airport.

———∞∞∞———

WHEN FATHER had walked me to the car, I slid into the backseat to find Mother already there, her large purse clutched in both hands. It was bulging, likely stuffed full of necessities for our trip, I thought, but as soon as the house was out of sight she zipped open the main pocket and pulled out her ratty coat. She picked at the knots in the fur collar and ran her fingers over the thick brass buttons and the one strange gold button on the bottom, smaller than the rest and stamped with a crown in the center.

I hadn't noticed the gold button before; in fact, I hadn't ever had the chance to look closely at the coat, because whenever Father sees it he threatens to incinerate the filthy thing if it ever appears in front of him again. Even still, whenever the newspaper runs an unflattering story about Father, whenever he reduces the pool boys to tears, whenever my sisters or I hurl creative insults at each other— basically, whenever Mother is upset about anything—she digs out that coat and won't take it off until fences (or newspaper presses, or pools) are mended. She had been carrying it around with her ever since she told me about Lily Brook.

"What's that?" I ran my finger over the button.

"Oh," Mother said, sniffing back her tears, her eyes lighting up. "My grandmother had a friend, an old man, who came to visit us sometimes in our cottage in the forest. He always wore a purple velvet suit, and I think this button," she said, smiling as she touched it, "was one of his."

My mother rarely talks about her time with her parents and grandmother in the little house in the forest. Her family died when she was four. A tree fell in the night and reduced their house to splinters, missing her own cot by only a hair. One of the woodcutters her father worked with found her sitting in the dirt the next morning, wrapped in her grandmother's coat, and took her to the orphanage his wife worked in to have her cleaned up and fed. She arrived just as a Boston coal magnate and his wife were leaving, dissatisfied with the selection of orphans there were to choose from. The wealthy couple took one look at my mother—her long brown curls, her large dark eyes—and chose her immediately. And even though they hadn't really meant for her to be given away, the woodcutter and his wife decided that this was best for her, the opportunity to be brought up in a rich family.

My mother claims she remembers all this: the lightning strike that sent the tree crashing through the cottage roof, her parents and grandmother trapped beneath the thick trunk, the conversation between the woodcutter and his wife in the doorway of the orphanage before they placed my mother in the back of the rich couple's car. She doesn't remember other details—the name of the place she was born, for instance, or whether it is close to Currency or miles away. Her new family refused to speak about her life before she became their daughter.

Father also hates it when Mother talks about her pre-Boston life. Poverty is dirty, he says, and always adds that he married Mother despite her humble beginnings, certainly not because of them. With that, he'll usually push out a laugh and grab her in a bone-crushing hug, as if he were only joking. It's clear, though, that he never is.

In the car to the airport, Mother stared into her lap, stroking the arm of her coat. "I've heard wonderful things about Lily Brook, Danny. The quality of instruction is beyond compare, the facilities are exceptional, the setting is stunning. You're bound to have a fabulous time there. Still …" She reached for my hand again and squeezed it hard, her fingernails cutting moon-shaped grooves into my palm. "I can't help thinking that my Granny would turn over in her grave if she knew we were sending you away.

"She was an orphan too, you know," she said in a whisper, glancing quickly behind us. "This coat was really her father's. His name was Zuther, just like your middle name." She smiled, then leaned in closer. "I told your father a 'Zuther' was a foreign currency so he would agree to sign your birth certificate, but you were named after your great-great-grandfather. That's our little secret, Danny." She winked, and then burst into tears again.

When she managed to stop, she pulled at the gold button until it popped free, pressed it to her lips, and then placed it in my hand.

⸺◦◦◦⸺

I AM CLUTCHING THE BUTTON, whispering my middle name—my great-great-grandfather's name—when Mr. Remroddinger raises his voice to a shout.

"For the final time, Emily Rose Buckler. Present or not present?"

The room is silent.

Mr. Remroddinger glances at his pocket watch and mutters something under his breath. He shakes his head and wipes invisible beads of sweat from his scrunched-up forehead. As he does, there is a knock on the door. One of the uniformed women slides back the bolt and wedges the door open a crack.

"Is this where we're to meet for Lily Brook?" asks a girl's bright voice. Her face is pressed against the crack so that a sliver of nose and a slice of ear are visible.

"Emily Buckler," calls Mr. Remroddinger from across the room. "Are you alone?"

"Yes, sir, I sure am," answers the voice.

"Then hurry up; time is wasting."

The women in gray pull the door open just far enough for Emily to squeeze through, then shut it tightly and draw the bolt again. Emily Buckler flops into the seat that Mother has just left, and shifts from side to side, examining the room. She is a tall black girl, with large bony kneecaps that poke out from below the hem of her skirt. Her hair is pulled into frizzy pigtails.

When she stops fidgeting, her gaze lands first on me, then on José. She grins at us both. "This will be fun, hey?"

José snorts.

"What's eating him?"

I shrug without making eye contact; I am focusing on what Mr. Remroddinger is saying, and focusing even harder on the glass door behind him, trying to decide how easy it would be to escape. One of the women in the back cracks her knuckles and the sound is like a broom handle being snapped in two. I decide against running.

"Emily Buckler." Emily extends her long thin fingers out towards me. "Average daughter of Sandhill Buckler—cocoa powder tycoon—and his glamorous wife, Elsa."

I nod, then lean forward, straining towards the podium.

"And you are?" Emily jerks her head, motioning towards her still-outstretched hand.

"Danny Chandelier." I shake her hand quickly, but keep my eyes on Mr. Remroddinger. He seems to be finished with attendance and is now shoving papers into his briefcase.

"Oh, sure," Emily grins. "Walkerton Chandelier. You got sisters, right? I've read all about them in Mom's articles. She keeps a file on each man on the continent richer than Daddy," she adds. "I've never heard of you, though, Danny Chandelier, but I guess that's why you're here, right? You and me and the rest of these kids, a handful of pits floating in the cherry jam."

Ever since Mother showed me the Lily Brook brochure, I've spent a lot of time thinking about how average I am, and how exceptional my sisters are in comparison. And every time I think about it, I feel miserable. But Emily is beaming, as if being ordinary is some kind of wonderful gift. I wonder when she realized she wasn't as special as her family. Maybe the rest of the kids here knew all along how regular they were. But I had never thought that my sisters were better than me, more interesting and important, until the Lily Brook brochure pointed it out.

IV

MR. REMRODDINGER SNAPS HIS BRIEFCASE SHUT and strides over to the uniformed women; he whispers something, then pulls out his pocket watch again and glances at it. The women lean towards him and nod, but they don't take their eyes off us for even an instant. The room is silent, except for the creaking of Emily Buckler's chair—she's pumping her legs like she's on a swing set and is expecting to become airborne at any moment. I try to ignore her and stay focused on Mr. Remroddinger. What is he saying? Caroline and I used to mouth words to each other when we were younger—lip-reading practice, she said. Useful against parents and teachers. I'm trying to read Mr. Remroddinger's lips when

Emily leans in close and jabs my side with her finger.

"What do you think the best part will be?" She's not even trying to keep her voice down, and I can feel every pair of eyes in the room staring in our direction.

"It's hard to narrow it down to one thing, isn't it?" she continues, when I don't respond. "On the one hand, I'm really excited about the classes. I've never studied Latin before, or metallurgy, and I can't wait for astronomy lessons. I expect we'll get to use real telescopes and we'll learn the names of all the constellations. But then, the extracurriculars sound thrilling too: scuba diving, circus arts, ice climbing …. Probably, though, the best part will be making new friends, don't you think?" She motions towards the tear-stained faces surrounding us. "Already everyone seems so nice."

Beside her, José snorts and mutters something under his breath. He has a drawing spread out on his lap, and he's tracing the felt pen lines with his finger.

Emily turns to him. "What are you most looking forward to?"

"Leaving." He doesn't look up when he says it, but continues staring into his lap.

"I agree; once we board that plane the adventure will begin!" Emily claps her hands as if she can hardly contain her excitement. "I've been counting down the hours."

"I've been counting down too," José snorts. "Five years and ten months until I graduate and get the heck out of Poplovastan."

At first Emily doesn't respond, but then she leans

towards me and whispers, "He's probably not always this grumpy. I expect he just misses his family." But before I can respond she has turned back to José.

"Did someone draw that for you?"

He doesn't answer, only folds the picture in half and then half again.

"*We love and miss you, from Maya and Celia.* Who are Maya and Celia? Are they your friends?"

For the first time, José looks up at Emily. He narrows his eyes at her in a terrifying glare.

But Emily is undaunted. "Your *girl* friends?" she teases.

"Sisters," he grumbles.

"That's so sweet. I have an older brother, but he must have forgotten I was leaving today. He and my parents are on a business trip, and their hotel phone is broken. They didn't answer it when I called. Can I see it again?"

When José unfolds the paper and angles it towards Emily, I glance at the drawing: a boy in a sparkly black outfit stands with his arms stretched over his head and one leg extended in a high kick.

"Is that supposed to be you? What are you doing?" Emily reaches for the paper, but when she grabs it, José yanks it away. There's a ripping noise, and Emily is left holding onto a jagged corner.

Emily and José both stare at the piece of paper pinched between her fingers. "Sorry," she says. "I ..." But she doesn't get a chance to finish. José jumps up from his seat and stomps across the room, where he slumps into a chair pushed against the opposite wall.

Emily is still staring at the piece of paper in her hand. Slowly, she places it on the seat José has just vacated. Maybe it's my imagination, but it seems like her chin has started to quiver.

Mother has a way of cheering up everyone around her, even strangers. If she were here, she'd place her hand on Emily's shoulder and tell her not to worry. She'd ask Emily questions about herself, or share a funny story— something to get her mind off things. I stick my hand in my pants pocket and rub my thumb over the button's surface. Then I turn to Emily Buckler.

"Emily?"

Her eyes are wet and glossy, but she sets her mouth into a smile as she faces me.

"Have you ever met anyone who went to Lily Brook?"

"No," she says quietly, but then the excitement returns to her voice. "But my dad knows someone whose son is there, and he just loves it. He's always writing letters home and he says he never wants to leave."

"Does he mention the food?" A slightly pudgy boy in the next row is leaning towards us, his bright green eyes fixed on Emily. "Is it satisfactory?"

"Probably," Emily says. "He didn't say it was bad, anyway."

"Still …" The boy looks concerned. "I'd like to know. I prefer that ingredients are sourced locally, but no one I've asked seems aware of Poplovastan's main crops. And the brochure didn't say anything about access to kitchen facilities."

"You cook?" As soon as I ask, I realize it's a pretty dumb question. On his lap, the boy is holding a large metal toolbox with a padlock on the front. In red paint across the top are the words "Trevor's Spice Cabinet— Handle with Extreme Care."

The boy shrugs. "I spend a lot of time in the test kitchen of my family's restaurant. I like to experiment."

"What restaurant?" Emily asks.

"You probably haven't heard of it."

"Maybe I have."

Trevor yawns and raises his hand to his mouth, and when it's there—covering his lips from view—he mutters something that sounds to me like "Buggo Uggo." But Emily obviously understands him.

"I love Biggo Burger! There are three of them on my street! Which do you think is better—the Big Slugger Steak or the Big Chief Chicken?"

"Neither." Trevor's stomach gurgles and he rubs it through his cable-knit sweater. "I'm not really the fast-food type. I've tried to improve the Biggo menu. I've come up with all sorts of gourmet burgers: lamb marinated in an orange-mint sauce, grilled portobello mushroom with roasted red peppers … my dad won't even try them. He says nothing in the world tastes better than Biggo's Biggest Beef."

"Are you hungry right now?" Emily has zipped open the front pocket of her suitcase and is pulling out striped knee socks and woolen tights, apparently looking for something.

"I'm *always* hungry." As if to prove his point, his stomach lets out another loud rumble.

"You'll love this. My cook Louisa's famous chocolate chip cookies." Emily pulls a pink tin from her suitcase. "She has a secret ingredient."

Trevor takes the cookie Emily is holding out and brings it to his nose. "Instant coffee," he says. "Probably just a teaspoon per batch." He takes a small bite and closes his eyes, chewing slowly. "Definitely. That's her secret ingredient."

Emily doesn't seem to hear him. Tucked into the side of the cookie tin is a small white recipe card, and she pulls it out. *My dear, sweet Emily,* I read, before looking away.

After a moment, Emily slips the recipe card into her pocket and stands up. She proceeds to walk along the rows of chairs, introducing herself to all the other kids and offering them cookies from her tin. When she reaches José, he won't look at her, but she takes the final two cookies and places them on his lap.

When Emily sits down again, a skinny man appears at the glass door behind the podium. "All aboard for Lily Brook," he calls. His pilot's cap is at least a size too large, and it's tilted down, covering half his face. That is the extent of his formal uniform. The sleeves of his yellow windbreaker are too short for his long bony arms, and his legs stick out from a pair of pilled gym shorts.

Mr. Remroddinger ushers us out the door and onto the tarmac. Waves of heat warble the highway in the distance, and the grass at the edge of the runway is crisp and brown. The first student out the door drops off his trunk beside the rusted luggage cart and walks towards the sleek silver plane positioned to the right of the building.

"Wrong one, wrong one." Mr. Remroddinger waves him back. But there is no other plane nearby except an old cargo jet with banged-up wings tilted halfway off the runway. It's painted blue and orange, but for a coat or two of white sloshed over the belly where the old company name "Grandpa Jake's Flaky Cakes" is still visible underneath. The pilot walks towards it and up the ladder that leads to the door, trailed by the two women in gray.

"He's not serious," one of the girls beside me whispers. But he looks to be serious. The pilot pauses at the top of the ladder and motions for us to follow.

"Hop to it now; we've hardly any time to lose. I get paid by the delivery, not by the hour."

As I climb the rickety steps to the door of the cargo plane, Mr. Remroddinger wheels a small suitcase across the tarmac towards the silver plane beside us.

"Have a pleasant flight, children," he calls, before ducking aboard.

V

IT WAS MOTHER who showed me the brochure, but Lily Brook was obviously my father's idea. He was the one who took Mr. Remroddinger's hand that night he arrived in our hallway. Took it and pumped it hard, up and down and up and down. Mr. Remroddinger reminded me of a fat black fly discovering a pile of Archduke Pooch's poop in the grass. He was wide-eyed and greedy-looking in his smarmy blazer, sizing up my sisters' jewelry, my father's bulging wallet pocket, and I could tell that in his head he was rubbing his hands together in delight.

My mother went into Father's office to speak to Mr. Remroddinger too, but before she did, she came up behind me and ruffled my hair. She wrapped her arms around my stomach and squeezed me into a hug from behind. Sometimes when I remember it, I think that when her face brushed the back of my neck it was wet with tears, but I can't be sure. I just know that the next morning, when Mother called me into her bedroom to show me the brochure, she was draped in her grandmother's ratty coat. I knew as soon as I laid eyes on it that whatever was about to happen couldn't be good.

Mother's whole body was curled underneath the coat, with only her head visible. The dank smell of mangy fur filled the room. She darted a hand out to pass me something and then pulled it back underneath. "Lily Brook—For Future Residents," said the front of the glossy booklet.

Under the heading was a picture of several smiling people squeezed together around a large sign: "Welcome to Lily Brook."

"Are we moving?" Even then, I suspected it was something far worse than that, but I tried my best to remain hopeful.

She sniffed and shook her head, no, then reached down and flipped the brochure open to the center: "Lily Brook Academy: The First Step of Your Journey." There was a faded photograph, spread over both pages, of a large brick building that looked more like a castle than a school. Smaller pictures of smiling students dotted the page: a girl with protective goggles holding a chemistry tube, two boys playing basketball on an outdoor court, a group of students studying intently at a table stacked high with books.

"So it's some kind of boarding school?" Midas Millions Academy was a boarding school and I had been excited about the prospect of going there, just like my sisters. Even though the Academy was in Midasville, just down the block from the junior preparatory, they only came home for weekends and holidays, and always had plenty of things to brag about when they did.

Mother sat up and draped the coat over her lap, and then clutched my hand and began to whisper to me about Poplovastan. I have globes and atlases all over my room in Currency, but it was the first time I'd ever heard of the place—a country wedged between Asia and Europe, so tiny that on most maps the line that divides the two continents covers it almost completely. A grapefruit-sized lump formed in my throat as Mother sent me to retrieve an atlas from my bedside table, then marked my future home with the tip of her fingernail. But despite my initial shock, it also seemed like for once *I* was the one doing something important, and doing it first.

Each of my sisters had begged for the chance to study abroad, but Father had said that they were too young, and he couldn't be convinced otherwise. And though I knew I'd miss my family, there would certainly be advantages to being away.

For one thing, it had been bad enough following in my sisters' footsteps all through Chandelier Junior

Preparatory. I was the only person related to the school's founder without his name etched on one of the large gold trophies in the case outside the office, the only one without his photograph on the Honor Roll Wall of Fame at the back of the auditorium. Being seen dropping me off at the remedial school across the street from Midas Millions Academy would have devastated my father.

Perhaps at Lily Brook I could truly become a good student. Perhaps Father would be able to brag about me at the family Christmas party this year, instead of excusing himself and heading for drinks every time someone in the extended family mentioned my name.

"And when I come home for Christmas ..." I started to say, thinking about the stories I would be able to tell my sisters, the adventures I would recount.

"You won't be back for Christmas." Father had appeared in the doorway with a cell phone in each hand. He held them against his chest as he spoke. "Not this year. The school likes to make sure you've settled in before they give out holiday passes."

"Then Easter." It came out as a squeaky whisper.

"Easter." Mother squeezed my hand. "Easter sounds wonderful."

My father frowned at her. "Zara, don't go getting the kid's hopes up. I wouldn't count on Easter, Danny. Or spring break for that matter."

"Walkerton." My mother began frantically stroking the arm of her coat. "Please."

"We talked to Mr. Remroddinger together, Zara, and

you know as well as I do how to approach this. Be up front with the kid; tell it like it is. Look, son." He shoved the phones into holsters attached to his belt, then turned to me and clasped my shoulder. "We all know you're not exactly in the same league as your sisters. And the thing is, maybe …"

"Maybe you'll shine at Lily Brook." Mother's lips flashed a smile, but it didn't reach her eyes.

"Right." Father let go of my shoulder and started towards the bed. "And who knows, you might even choose to stay in Poplovastan after you graduate."

"Oh, Walkerton, don't be terrible." Mother burst into tears and Father sat down beside her. He lifted her coat off her lap with his pinched thumb and forefinger and dropped it in a heap on the floor. He patted Mother's knee briefly, and then pulled both phones free again, pressing one to each ear. He listened for a moment, then rolled his eyes and shook his head.

"I said sell all the shares!" he yelled into both phones at once. "Now!" He turned to me, frowned, as if confused to see me standing there, and then shooed me from the room. I picked up the Lily Brook brochure and headed to my own bedroom across the hall. There were tears forming in my eyes, but I brushed them away with my fists. I sat on my bed and opened the brochure to the last spread of pages: "Lily Brook: The Journey Continues."

"Your time at Lily Brook doesn't have to end when you graduate from Lily Brook Academy. Most grads choose to make a life for themselves in Lily Brook. True, the lifestyle of a Lily Brook resident is not the same as the lifestyle of his or her family members back home. Lily Brook graduates do not attend Oxford or Yale; they do not become physicists, rock stars, or politicians. They do not host fox hunts, own sports teams, or establish factories in the Third World. Nonetheless, they are content and satisfied with their lives in Lily Brook, which is much more than average people elsewhere could ever dream of."

Was I content? I thought I was, but maybe I shouldn't have been. Would my life be better if I were good-looking like Annabelle, or brilliant like Brittany, or athletic like Caroline? I felt the sting of tears in my eyes again and blinked them away. Then I flipped to the back cover and stared at the photograph of a young girl with messy brown hair and a crooked nose. She had a wide grin on her face, and I glared at her, wondering what she had to be so pleased about. Then I noticed the caption underneath the photograph. "Lily Brook," it read. "1965–1983."

VI

THE INSIDE OF THE PLANE bound for Poplovastan is even worse than the outside. Pieces of metal flap from the ceiling, the lights flicker on and off, and the seats are nothing but rows of bench seats stolen from dilapidated school buses or scrounged from junkyards and screwed into place on the floor. The uniformed women escort us inside in pairs, yanking the seatbelts tightly against our waists with hissed instructions that we are not to leave our seats during the flight, or else. No one dares to ask *or else what*; the cracking of the women's knuckles as they pound their thick fists into their palms is answer enough.

The plane is enormous, and the rows of bench seats— three across and five deep—take up only a small section.

In the rear is a narrow door with the word "Toilet" spray-painted across it in red letters, but other than a few stacks of boxes and some pieces of crumpled metal that were probably attached to the plane at some point, the back of the cabin is empty. The pilot is on his hands and knees beside one of the stacks of boxes, feeling around on the ground in front of him. Finally, he picks up a small, circular object and places it in his pocket. He removes a hammer from one of the boxes and heads through the orange beaded curtain into the cockpit. Even if the curtain weren't there, I wouldn't be able to see into the front of the plane. The view is blocked by two large corduroy recliners that are bolted to the floor. In them, the hulking women sit facing us, and for the first time since hearing about Lily Brook I feel lucky—Emily and I were assigned a seat in the second row rather than the first.

As soon as the plane begins its ascent, it begins to hum and rattle. The clattering doesn't stop, even during the stillest of moments, and when we hit turbulence our seats rock wildly. About an hour into the flight, one of the bench seats collapses under a pair of girls. There is no other place for them to sit, so they are forced to share already full seats. One of them squeezes in between Emily Buckler and me. A short mousy kid with thin lips and stringy brown hair, she sits with her head hanging down, occasionally using a scrunched-up tissue to wipe at the trickle of blood that runs from her ankle onto her sock. In her other hand she clutches a ragged stuffed rabbit, whose ears she rubs against her cheeks.

There are no windows, but Emily amuses herself by imagining where we are and what it looks like below us.

"Strange there'd be this much turbulence over England," she whispers a few hours into the flight.

The mousy girl and I both look at the metal wall Emily is gazing at as if it were an actual window, but, of course, there is nothing to see.

"I suppose at this very moment they can see us from London Bridge," Emily continues.

"I do so love how lush the French countryside looks from above," she announces a little later. "Do you suppose Poplovastan will be lush, like it said in the brochure? I bet it'll be cold. But I love the winter. It's positively my favorite season."

"Do you have to be so cheerful?" José turns around from his seat in the first row and glares at Emily. "We are in a rickety old cargo plane, heading towards our deaths in some unpopulated hinterland. By the time anyone misses us enough to start a search, there'll be nothing left of us except a couple of bones the polar bears buried in the snow."

With that, the girl between Emily and me pulls the hood of her jacket on and cinches the drawstrings tight so her face is almost covered.

Emily strokes the girl's arm as if she were a lost and frightened kitten. "I never go with Mom and Dad when they vacation," she says. "My brother does, but not me. I stay home with our cook, Louisa. I'm not complaining; we always have a great time and all—spinning pizza dough on our fingers and making cakes just so we can lick the beaters. But it's nice that this time I'll have an adventure of my own. 'Lily Brook,'" she quotes. "'The adventure starts here.'"

"Don't make me vomit." José turns back around in his seat.

Emily pokes the girl between us. "You're Marcy Cooper, right? Daughter of Jim and Paige Cooper of J&P Cooper Infomercial Station: 'the station that's like a vacation.' You play the harp, you're an equestrian, and you wrote and illustrated a book of children's poetry. If you don't mind me asking, why are you here?"

The girl flips off her hood, but keeps her eyes on her lap. "I'm Maggie Cooper, Marcy's twin sister. I can't play anything, ride anything, or draw anything worth looking at." Her voice comes out in a whisper.

"Nice to meet you." Emily sticks out her hand.

Maggie turns to Emily. "I'm Maggie Cooper, not Marcy," she says a bit louder, without reaching for Emily's hand to shake.

"Exactly," Emily says, grabbing Maggie's hand from her lap and pumping it up and down. "It's nice to meet you, Maggie Cooper."

"It is?" Maggie asks. She looks startled. A smile flickers on her lips, but she bites it away. "People don't usually say that."

"You seem," Emily pauses, and gazes at Maggie, who stares hard at her stuffed rabbit. "You seem really kind. That's the best type of person to know, in my opinion."

Maggie's ears turn crimson and she doesn't answer. But when Emily grabs her arm and says, "I sure bet your sister is going to miss having you around," her eyes fill with tears. Big, silent tears that she rubs at with the furry paws of her stuffed rabbit. I don't know if I should say something or pretend not to notice; I hate it when people see me cry. After a moment I dig around in my jacket pocket for a tissue and place it on Maggie's lap.

"Thank you," she whispers. I glance at her, and she smiles. Her eyes are swollen and red, and the same ordinary brown as mine, but there's something else to them. Something that reminds me of Mother, something gentle. I smile back, and clutch the button in my fist.

AN HOUR OR SO AFTER Maggie wedges in between us, one of the women in gray passes out pencils and sheets of loose-leaf paper and instructs us to write a short essay about what we're most looking forward to at Lily Brook. I'm not looking forward to anything, and let my pencil slide around on the folding table the woman sets up in front of our seat. From the rattling around me, it's clear that most everyone else is doing the same.

Not Emily, though. She starts writing even before the table is in place, using Maggie's back as a flat surface, and then puts up her hand and asks for three extra sheets. I'm tempted to just hand my paper in blank, but the other woman opens a cardboard box and promises food when we're finished. I'm hungry enough to write a few sentences, which I steal word for word from the extracurricular section of the brochure—an enthusiastic spiel about swimming, horseback-riding, helicopter trips, and the go-kart track behind the school.

Once all the papers are in, snacks are doled out: two individually wrapped cupcakes each. A smiling farmer waves from the corners of the blue-and-orange packages. "Grandpa Jake" reads the rim of his straw hat. I wonder how long it's been since Grandpa Jake's Flaky Cakes owned this plane, and how long these cupcakes have been here. They are hardly "flaky"—in fact they are so stale they taste like chocolate-flavored sawdust.

The flight takes twelve hours, but the essay-writing and the eating of the cupcakes are our only diversions, aside from the seat collapsing under Maggie and the other girl, and Trevor being locked in the bathroom because he couldn't stop throwing up. Hardly anyone makes a sound the entire flight; hardly anyone can even be heard breathing, and after a while even Emily starts talking less and less and eventually not at all. Until the plane begins its descent, that is.

When the wings tip left and the nose tilts down, Emily hoots. "Poplovastan, here we come."

"Oh my goodness," she whispers to Maggie. "Can you believe it?"

"Believe what?" Maggie cranes her neck, but there's nothing to see.

"Why, the mountain, of course! It's enormous, it's

beautiful. It looks like a painting, so perfectly gray and blue and silver with snow on the top."

"Where are you looking?" Maggie sticks out her neck even further as the plane dips sharply down.

"And the forest, the beautiful forest, all those rich greens and browns. I wonder what kinds of animals live inside it. And that river, the rushing waters cutting through the fields." Emily's voice is getting louder and louder. A rumble of noise breaks out around us as everyone rustles to free themselves from their seatbelts and seek out the window that Emily must be gazing through.

My stomach drops and my hand shoots off my lap and starts feeling around my pocket before I know what it's doing. It finds the gold button and squeezes hard. The plane is tipping to one side and then the other, and Maggie bends over, her head pressed into her knees. I draw my own legs up into my chest. Every time my ears pop it feels like my head is exploding. Between the pops I can hear moaning, which seems to be coming from behind the bathroom door. I also hear Emily.

"The people." Emily's voice is raised almost to a shout. "Look at all the people, small as ants now, but I think … I'm almost certain … yes, I am certain. They're waving at us! They have welcome banners. The children are singing. Isn't it lovely? Isn't it just incredible?"

"Oh, yes, yes!" agree a couple of kids in the back, who obviously don't want to admit that they can't see what Emily sees.

"You're full of it." José slumps in his seat so just the tips of his spiked hair can be seen bobbing up and down every time the plane shifts.

I don't loosen my grip on the button even one little bit, and by the time the wheels touch down there is the shape of a crown pressed into my left palm.

VII

UNDER THE PHOTOGRAPH of Lily at the back of the brochure was a timeline, written in small black type.

1965: Richard and Gladys Brook's fifth child, Lily, is born.

1968: Lily fails to win the toddler beauty contest that each of her four siblings had won previously. While performing the gymnastics routine she trips and skins her knee on the stage. She is named eighth runner-up.

1969: Westingbrook Academy declares Lily's literacy skills average for a child her age and her hand-eye coordination in the bottom-third percentile. She is the first Brook child required to complete Kindergarten before registering in first grade.

1972: Lily's parents hire a Wimbledon champion to instruct their youngest daughter in daily tennis lessons. Lessons are discontinued when she is observed conceding defeat after a match against the housekeeper's son.

1975: Three presidents and eighteen dignitaries visit the Brooks' home for a formal dinner. Lily spills her milk on the lap of the President's wife and responds to a question about her future by announcing she will attend community college to become a veterinarian's assistant.

1979: Lily comes in twelfth in the National Private School Spelling Bee. She misspells the word "dividend," and while leaving the stage stumbles over her untied shoelaces.

1983: On a family air-balloon trip around Hawaii, Lily falls overboard into the mouth of a volcano. Her locket is found on a rock nearby. Inside is a note addressed to her family in which she cites their perfection and her inability to live up to it as the reason for ending her life. She is eighteen years old.

1983: For Lily's funeral, the Brooks request donations to the Lily Brook Foundation in lieu of flowers. Esteemed friends and business contacts donate a total of $13.4 million. The idea of Lily Brook Academy is born.

1984: The King of Poplovastan, a business associate of Richard Brook, offers to sell the Lily Brook Foundation a large tract of land, equal to 48 per cent of his country.

1985: Privileged families from around the world clog the phone lines when registration for Lily Brook Academy begins. All available spots are filled within thirty minutes.

1986: Lily Brook Academy opens.

1992: Students from the first graduating class claim they cannot bear to leave. Work commences to turn Lily Brook from a school into a community. Each year the town of Lily Brook expands.

Today: Now *you* have the opportunity to attend Lily Brook!

BEFORE I FOUND OUT about Lily Brook Academy, it had never occurred to me that my parents might be ashamed of me. Reading the brochure cover to cover that day in my bedroom, while I listened to Mother sob and Father grumble from across the hall, for the very first time I suspected that they were. I remembered the time the photographer from the *Post* had asked to take a picture of the four Chandelier children with their instruments after Brittany won the composition category of the national music festival when she was ten.

I came down the stairs with my ukulele, and Mother handed me my sheet music for "Mele Kalikimaka," the piece I was practicing to play for Father at Christmas. It was the first full-length song I had learned. But when Father saw me walking towards him with my ukulele tucked under my arm, he laughed, as if I had made a terribly funny joke, and turned to the photographer. "What a sense of humor the boy has," he said, as he thrust a twisted metal contraption half the size of my body, and twice as heavy, at me.

"What's this?" I tried to heave the thing over my shoulder, but could barely lift it from the ground.

"Seriously, Danny." My father smiled at the man over my head, but when he looked at me his eyes flashed a glare that burned my face. "Take your tuba and go sit with your sisters."

THE CHRONOLOGY OF LILY BROOK got me thinking about my own chronology a little. On the bookshelf in the hall Mother has a stack of scrapbooks for each of my sisters, stuffed with newspaper clippings about their various accomplishments. Propped up beside them is a thin green book with "Danny" written across the front. The day before I flew to Lily Brook, I retrieved it and took it to my room. Taped to the inside cover was a yellowing copy of my birth announcement from the newspaper. Well, not *my* birth announcement, exactly.

"I looked just like Annabelle did when I was born," I had said to my mother one day when she was showing my sisters and me the books. We had the same button noses and wisps of curls, the same long eyelashes and dimpled cheeks.

From beside me on the couch, Annabelle glanced over my shoulder.

"That *is* me," she said, and then went back to gazing at the baby beauty pageant clippings spread in front of her.

"Is not." I turned to Mother for reinforcement.

Mother squeezed my hand. "The photo may be of your sister, but the words are about you. Proud parents Zara and Walkerton. We sure were proud, Danny. You were a lovely little boy."

"Well, not quite, Mother." Annabelle reached over and flipped to the second page of my scrapbook, revealing my actual baby picture. It didn't take much to understand why Father hadn't allowed that photo to go to press. My entire body was covered in a puffy rash, from my bumpy bald head to the tips of my sausage-shaped toes. "You looked like a gremlin until you were four."

Through the corner of my eye I could see Mother shake her head sharply at my sister.

"You know," Annabelle said, searchingly, "so ugly you were almost cute."

———∞———

I THUMBED FORWARD a few pages in the scrapbook and stopped at a photocopy of my painting entitled *Chocolate Butterfly*. The original still hangs in Mother's dressing room. I remember how proud she was when she first saw it, how she told Father she was certain I had an artistic gift. She had him submit the painting to the international preschooler art exhibition. But when the curator came to the house to inspect my artwork, he told Father I would never be a success. Mother had argued with him. My painting was fantastic. What did he know?

"Are you claiming to be an expert in the field, Mrs. Chandelier?" The curator started for the door in a huff, and Father's neck flushed pink. He apologized for my mother, for both of us, and practically shoved us from the room.

I flipped over a couple more pages until I came to the sheet music for "Baby Beluga." Glued beside it was a photograph of me in first grade. I was wearing thin red suspenders and my mouth was wide open; likely I was singing at the top of my lungs. Mother and I sang "Baby Beluga" everywhere: in the car, at the grocery store, when she tucked me into bed. The picture in the book was probably taken just before the school principal told Father my singing was a distraction to the other students. It disrupted their chess games and poetry discussions. Father then banned all children's music from the household and replaced it with recordings of violin concertos.

There were plenty of things the scrapbook didn't show. Like the time Archduke Pooch (the first) died and I packed up his toys and gave them to the woman who sat outside the bank downtown with her cocker spaniel. Father was horrified when I hugged "the filthy mutt" and he covered the back seat with newspaper before he would let me get back in the car. At first his only instruction to Isabella was to draw me a bath and add a capful of bleach to the water, but then he found me lying on his and Mother's bed in my pajamas, scratching at my scalp as Mother rubbed calamine lotion on my arms and legs. She said the bleach was the culprit, not fleas, but Father still confined me to the servants' wing for a week. Mother didn't make me stay there, though, and Father never knew the difference—

he had checked himself into a hotel for the duration.

What about the empty page that could have held ribbons from the relay team, if only Father had let me run? I was the fourth-fastest runner at Chandelier Junior Preparatory last year and was awarded the second leg of the relay team for the district competition. But Father wouldn't hear of it. He demanded that I run the anchor leg, or at the very least the starter leg. "Second leg?" He had cornered the headmaster in the school hallway and bellowed at him: "The grandson of the school's founder should cross the finish line, not be left stranded in the center of the track! I hope, dear sir, your suggestion was intended as a joke." But it wasn't a joke, and when the track coach said second leg or no leg, my father refused to let me run at all.

Or what about the family vacation to Estonia, only last year? After weeks of language lessons my sisters impressed Father's new business contacts by discussing European politics, post-modernist art, and the weather. When I tried to ask the ambassador to pass the salt I ended up telling him his nose was bigger than an elephant's. Father made Isabella—who had been standing in the hallway during our meal, as usual—walk me back to the hotel room to prevent any further embarrassment.

What would Mother put in her scrapbook next? My rejection letters from Midas Millions? A few stray, shredded remains of the brochure for my new boarding school in the middle of nowhere?

Maybe the rest of the pages would just stay blank.

VIII

POPLOVASTAN IS nothing like the window in Emily's head made it out to be. There is a shocked silence as we begin to file out of the plane, down the steps, and onto the tarmac. Maybe most of us actually expected to see the mountain, the forest, the river, the people with banners, and the singing children. Instead we see almost nothing at all. It is pitch-black out, and except for a floodlight shining on a small red shack beside us with "Terminal" spray-painted on the door, all of Poplovastan is in the dark. There are no city lights in the distance, no sounds of cars on a nearby freeway. Only thick, black night.

The two women in gray herd us through the terminal doors. The building is a small square room with stark white walls, a concrete floor, and a single flickering light bulb hanging from the ceiling. There is no furniture except for a cluster of metal chairs near the far wall. And filling each of them is a large adult in a stiff gray uniform, frowning at us. A couple of them lean back in their seats and flex their bulging muscles under the sleeves of their shirts. One of the women sits flicking pieces of food from her teeth with a metal skewer, and the man beside her twist the ends of his mustache into sharp points. Some of the girls start to cry. Some of the boys start to cry. A grown man starts to cry.

"But, please." The pilot is trying to drag a uniformed man towards the exit. "I need the plane gassed up immediately. You can't possibly expect me to spend another night in Lily Brook."

The uniformed man peels the pilot's fingers off his arm, and the pilot tries again. Whimpering, he clutches the wrist of a sour-looking blond woman and pulls her towards the door. I'm so intent on watching him that I don't notice another hulking figure enter the terminal until she reaches the front of the room.

"Attention, you rich little brats, you varmints, you good-for-nothing sacks of noodles." She's wearing the same uniform as the rest, except that her pants are tucked into a pair of black leather army boots that reach almost to her knees. She has a red beret pulled down over her eyebrows and tipped slightly to the side, and in matching red thread the word "Captain" is embroidered on her shirt pocket.

And she is large. Terribly large—tall and solid, with a build like a gorilla. Her legs and neck are thicker than telephone poles and her bright orange hair is twisted into a braid that reaches halfway to the floor. The room is silent, except for the whip-like crack of the woman's braid every time she turns her head, and the loud popping noises when she cracks her knuckles. I try to pull my eyes away from her enormous hands, but when I look up at her face the sight is even more terrifying. A scar runs from the edge of her right eye to the corner of her lip, and when she smiles—revealing a row of sharp yellow teeth—the scar quivers, like a snake about to strike. Even Emily Buckler, pressed against the back wall with her eyes fixed on the woman, looks terrified.

"Welcome," the woman says. "To Lily Brook. I am Elmira Maria Despera. You may *not* call me Elmira. You may not call me Ms. Despera. You may not call me Ma'am. You *will* call me Captain Ma'am. You might forget my name the first time you address me, but I can assure you, you will not forget it the second time."

Captain Ma'am stops talking and focuses her beady eyes on a boy in the doorway. He's facing the airstrip. "What are you looking for?"

Everyone is silent. The girl standing closest to the back-turned boy jabs him in the side with her elbow. Slowly, he turns around.

"Nothing, Captain Ma'am," the boys answers in a whisper.

"I expect you're looking for Lily Brook Academy,

with its castle turrets and fine stained-glass windows."

The two guards from the airplane burst out laughing. One of them has to lean against the wall, clutching her stomach, until she catches her breath. Tears stream down her cheeks and her teeth are bared in a wild white grin.

"Or maybe," Captain Ma'am continues, "it's the horses you're looking for, or the lake? The crowds of smiling people?" A man in the doorway hoots a laugh, but with a look from Captain Ma'am he bites his lip and looks down at his shiny boots.

"Oh, there will be plenty to see come morning, you soggy pancakes, you little vermin."

Just then a thin voice pipes up from the back of the room. "When my father hears how I've been treated …"

Captain Ma'am starts to laugh. It's a wicked laugh, a deep and gurgling laugh. Her belly jiggles and she rocks back and forth on the heels of her enormous boots. Then the uniformed women from our flight start to laugh again, and a couple of the uniformed men sitting beside them join in until the room is filled with screeches, like the jackals' den in the Midasville Zoo.

"When my father hears how I've been treated," mimics the man beside Captain Ma'am, in a fake squeaky voice.

Captain Ma'am stops laughing. She stops smiling. Instantly, all the men and women stop laughing. All I can hear is my blood pulsing in my head.

"Your father," Captain Ma'am points one thick finger at the boy who interrupted her, "will not hear about this. *Your* father," she jabs her finger towards a small boy in the front row, "will not hear about this. Not *your* father, or *your* father, or *your* father." She points at kid after kid. "Nor will your mothers, or brothers, or sisters, or aunts, or cousins, or goldfish, and you know why not?"

No one makes a sound.

"I said, do you know why not?"

"Why not, Captain Ma'am?" asks Emily Buckler from the back of the room. She's standing up tall now and has her arms folded across her chest.

"I'm glad you asked, young lady." Captain Ma'am narrows her eyes and looks directly at the boy who first spoke. "Your family will not hear about this because they will not ask. They will not ask because they do not care. In the twenty years since Lily Brook's opening, not one measly parent, not one single rich twit, has even so much as sent a letter. And judging by the look of you sorry lot," she turns her head slowly, glancing from one of us to the next, her expression twisting from disgust to utter repulsion, "there are certainly no pity parties in progress back where you came from."

"Now," she says, clapping her hands and shaking her head, as if to dislodge the sickening vision of us from her brain, "the longer we're here, the less sleep you get, and believe me, with what tomorrow has in store for you, you'll be wishing you'd hit the hay hours ago. I want you to split yourself into six equal groups—the Twits, the Nits, the Half-Wits, the Dimwits, the No-Wits, and the Uglies. Chop chop." She claps her hands again. I look around, waiting for someone else to move, but no one does. The room is silent, and when I blink my eyes the sound of my eyelids hitting together seems to echo off the walls. Then:

"Hey, Danny," someone calls from across the terminal. "Want to be in my group?" I know without even looking that it's Emily Buckler.

"Okay …" I try to say as I turn around, but no sound comes. A couple of other people start to shift towards each other. Maggie joins us and so does Trevor. Actually, he doesn't so much join us as stay where he is, curled on the floor by Emily's feet, holding his stomach. Soon there's silence again, except for the shuffling of feet and a couple of hushed whispers.

"I see," says Captain Ma'am, "that you ragamuffins, you wormy potatoes, you lumpy loafers, are going to have a harder time than I thought. Thirty divided by six is five, and I see very clearly one group of six and one group of four." Captain Ma'am begins to stride over to the far corner of the room. There's shoving and pushing as everyone in the group of six tries to eject someone other than themselves. In the end José is hurtled towards Captain Ma'am. He prevents himself from barreling into her by performing a sideways leap that looks positively acrobatic.

"Very good." She catches him by the ear and drags him across the room until she's standing in front of our group. "Now, this group," she says, glaring at us appraisingly, "are most obviously the Uglies. And you, you little bug-eyed brute, are a perfect fit." She gives him a push towards us, but José digs his heels into the floor and doesn't move an inch. He points at Emily. "Please don't put me with her, Ma'am."

Suddenly, the uniformed guards, who have been muttering and mumbling to one another, go silent. They peer at our group, smiling and rubbing their hands together. I feel my breath catch in my throat.

"What did you call me?"

José's ears flush red and a slow trickle of sweat runs down his forehead and splashes onto one lens of his glasses.

"Captain Ma'am," he croaks. "I said Captain Ma'am."

"Come with me, you cross-eyed crawly." She grabs him by a tuft of hair and drags him towards the exit. By the time the rest of the guards line us up and march us outside, he is nowhere in sight and our group is down to four again.

There are six rusty mail trucks on the slab of concrete in front of the terminal, and each group is herded into the back of one. One of the guards, a short, stocky black man with incredibly tiny hands and feet and a brush cut that makes his gray hair look as sharp as steel wool, corrals Trevor, Emily, Maggie, and I into the truck at the end of the line. Once we're all seated on the bench against the sidewall, he stands in the doorway and snarls at us. Behind him, a thin woman, with skin so pale it seems to glow in the moonlight, stands with her hands on her hips and narrows her icy blue eyes. The man spits on the ground beside his tiny feet and slams the door. Moments later the engine starts.

"You still think this is an adventure?" Trevor asks Emily, who is whistling show tunes under her breath.

"You never know what's in store for us out there," Emily says, but, squished against her on the narrow bench, I can feel her legs shaking.

IX

WHEN I STEP from the back of the truck I feel a flood of relief. What appears to be in store for us at Lily Brook is not as bad as I'd feared. Directly in front of me is a large stuccoed house with green painted shutters and door. The curtains are drawn over the windows but the lights are on, so a faint glow escapes through the glass, illuminating the window boxes full of red geraniums.

I begin to walk up the path, but as soon as I do a heavy hand, belonging to the uniformed man from our truck, grips my shoulder.

"You think I'd let you sleep in my bed, Ugly?" He twists me around until I face the other direction, and the relief I felt only moments before quickly curdles, turning to sheer dread.

We are standing at the far end of a cement parking lot, with dozens of rusted mail trucks, like the one we took from the airport, parked in every direction. On the other side of the lot, six buildings loom in the shadows. Each has a light on the side, and under the light, a painted sign: Twits, Nits, Half-Wits, Dimwits, No-Wits, and Uglies. The man gives me a push, and I start off towards the final building, a concrete rectangle without a single window. Trevor, Emily, and Maggie tuck in close to me.

"We are the guards of this complex," booms the man from the darkness behind us. "Your house parents." He snorts out a laugh.

The pale woman, now walking in front of us, stops and turns around. She points a finger to her chest.

"And for this reason," the man says, "you will refer to my associate here as Mother Ma'am." Mother Ma'am glares at us when he says this and nods her head vigorously.

"You can call me Bob."

Mother Ma'am pulls keys from her pocket and clicks open the padlock attached to the door handle. She ushers us inside and Bob follows, slamming the door behind him. The muggy air—heavy with the smell of sweaty socks and mildew, dust and stale breath—surrounds me. But I can't tell where the smell is coming from—it's even darker inside than out.

I think about my room in Currency—the aquariums of snails and newts on my windowsill, Archduke Pooch II's mattress on the floor beside my bed, the family photo—taken last Christmas—in a silver frame over my desk. I think of the thick blue carpet, and the soft green cotton sheets. The smell of Mother's hand cream on the pages of my books from the nights she read them to me aloud. I would give anything to be back there. In fact, I would give anything to be anywhere else. I take a step forward and knock my shin against something hard.

Just then, from deep in the darkness, there's a loud sneeze.

But that isn't the only noise. I hold my breath and let the sounds slip through my ears. There is heavy breathing all around us. There is wheezing, sniffling, snoring, and mumbling. I'm straining to see what's in front of me, when suddenly the room is bathed in dingy yellow light. A single bulb hangs by a frayed wire from the center of the ceiling. It sways back and forth, sending the shadows rushing towards us before they retreat into the corners.

Now I can see where the noises are coming from—in the space in front of us are bunk beds, two rows of them, with a narrow path in between. There must be close to thirty beds all together, each leaning, towering, shifting with sleeping bodies. Some are two bunks high, some three, and some are even four—the top mattress just inches from the ceiling. Bob points to a rickety double bunk bed close to the door. There are spikes sticking out from the sides and a pile of sawdust at the base. The mattresses, lumpy and hard-looking, have springs poking from them.

"Ladies first," he sneers.

As soon as Maggie and Emily have crawled into their beds, Bob leads Trevor and me towards a thick black curtain that hangs from the ceiling just beyond the cluster of bunks full of female Uglies. He pulls the edge of it back to reveal a grid of thick iron bars and, beyond them, a replica of the room we just walked through.

When he has unlocked the padlock by the wall and slid the bars back just enough for Trevor and me to squeeze past them, he points to a wobbly three-story bunk in front of us, then slams the bars shut and pulls the curtain closed. We have just enough time to scramble into bed—Trevor below, me squeezed into the tight space of the middle bunk—before the light is switched off. The mattress caves under my weight and a spring pushes against my kidney. The pillow is damp and woodsy-smelling. I reach under my head to fluff it, and my hand grabs a pile of sawdust. The third bunk is only inches from my nose and I hope that when José arrives, *if* José arrives, it won't splinter under his weight and crush me to death.

Or maybe it would be better if it did. Because from what I've seen of Lily Brook so far, death by collapsing bunk bed might be preferable.

"Sleep tight." Bob's voice booms from somewhere in the darkness. "Don't forget to let the bedbugs bite."

The door slams and there is a click as the deadbolt is locked. Trevor starts to moan. Through the curtain I can hear someone whistling a lullaby. Trust Emily.

"HEY," A VOICE CALLS from the darkness. "Welcome to the Uglies."

The room comes to life with noise.

"Umph."

"Ouch."

"Coming down."

"My fingers!"

"Whoops, sorry"

"Umph."

A flashlight switches on. It bobs around the far side of the room. Pretty soon it and its carrier—a tall thin man with a shock of white hair and a thick white beard—come towards us. The man is followed by a swarm of others, clusters of moving shadows pushing down the rows of beds to end up in the space surrounding our bunks. The curtain is tugged back and a row of faces greets us through the bars—a dazed Maggie and a grinning Emily among them.

"I'm Ernst, Ernst Hefflebauer." The flashlight carrier addresses himself to both sides of the metal grid. "People here call me Uncle Ernst." He sticks out his hand to Trevor, then up to me, then pushes it between the bars to shake with Emily and Maggie.

"Hey." Emily squints and points her finger at the man. "Just a second. Hefflebauer, huh? You don't happen to be any relation to Max Hefflebauer do you? Household utensil magnate, founder of Hefflebauer's

Super Strength Spatulas Incorporated."

"Well, I'll be." Uncle Ernst shakes his head and grins. "Max Hefflebauer's my brother … spatulas, eh? Isn't that something. Max was only knee-high to a spatula himself when I was shipped off to Lily Brook."

"Max Hefflebauer," Emily is saying. "Married, one daughter, enjoys sailing and sampling wine from his vineyard. Only brother deceased in a plane crash at twelve years of age."

"You don't say." Uncle Ernst whistles a sigh through his teeth. "Deceased in a plane crash, howd'ya like that? And what's your name, child?"

"I'm Emily Buckler, sir, daughter of Sandhill Buckler, cocoa magnate. Pleased to make your acquaintance. My family's cook, Louisa, she's a real big fan of the spatulas. She's always telling me how sturdy they are, and how pretty they are to look at. One Halloween when I was little she made me a fairy costume, with a pink spatula for a wand." Emily's voice gets softer, and in the dim beam of the flashlight her eyes look wet. She sniffs and rubs her nose with her sleeve. "So it's an honor, really, to meet you."

"Well, now." Uncle Ernst steps closer to the bars. "Miss Emily Buckler. You sure are chipper for a fresh-off-the-plane Lily Brooker. Didn't they give you the full treatment? Twelve hours of turbulence, Captain Ma'am and all her hooting and hollering, the teeth-rattling ride in the mail truck over the rocks and potholes?"

"They sure did." Emily takes out her hair elastics and runs her fingers through her braids—dislodging a large clump of sawdust.

"Hey." A woman pushes up close to Maggie, then squints at Trevor and me through the bars. She's ancient-looking, with a heavily creased face and a frizz of white hair. "There are only four of you. Didn't they say five, Ernst? Five new Uglies?"

"There *are* five of us," I say. "José, he's the fifth. But he called Captain Ma'am just plain Ma'am and she—"

"He didn't." From behind me there are a few loud gasps.

"Oh, how horrid," cries a balding man to my right.

"And on his first day." A thin-faced woman next to Emily shakes her head.

"And she took him out behind the terminal," I continue.

"Oh, yes." Uncle Ernst places his hand on my shoulder. "No need to go on, son. We all know what she did to him."

"What *did* she do to him?" Trevor asks.

There is silence. Not even the sound of breath.

"Well, you see." A wiry man with a thick gray beard pushes between Trevor and me. "You see, children ..."

"Yes, well," Uncle Ernst interrupts. "Perhaps not on your first night. There will be time for such tales later, when you have, well, when you have adjusted to your surroundings."

"Have you really been here since you were twelve?" Maggie's voice is a squeaky whisper.

"Oh, yes." Ernst nods his head solemnly. "I was in the first group of Lily Brook residents. There are usually thirty newcomers a year, that's five in each building. This year is the twentieth year, which means there should be six hundred in all, one hundred per building. Except ..." He pauses, then lowers his voice. "Some of our members are no longer with us. So there's just over five hundred Lily Brook Residents in all, not counting the guards and the Royals. Including you children and your missing friend, we Uglies number eighty-three."

"No longer with you?" A small smile quivers onto Trevor's face. "Do you mean they got to go home?"

"Er ... not home, exactly."

"Twenty years?" I calculate Uncle Ernst's age in my head. "So you're only thirty-two?"

"Just turned," Uncle Ernst replies. "I was an August baby."

"Twenty years," I repeat softly.

"I know," whispers a man behind me. His face is a combination of sharp angles—jutting cheekbones, sharp chin. He looks like he is Mother's age, perhaps slightly older. "Can you imagine?"

"Have you been here that long too?"

"Me?" he snorts. "Of course not; I'm only thirteen. A year ago today I was a newbie myself."

"But that's ..." I start to say, but then I think better

of it. In the beam of light from Uncle Ernst's flashlight, all the Lily Brookers look much older than they must be. In fact, we seem to be the only children in a room full of worn and tired adults. Most of the men are balding, some of the women have hair peppered with gray, and others have hair as white as Uncle Ernst's. Almost all of the faces staring at us are cut with wrinkles, and patches dark as bruises circle their tired eyes. Is this what life at Lily Brook does to people? I decide to change the topic.

"Who are the Royals?"

"That you will soon discover, my boy," answers Uncle Ernst. "Now try to catch some sleep, children. Morning always comes much too soon to Lily Brook."

X

MORNING DOES COME much too soon. In fact, it seems like I've just closed my eyes when the light begins flickering and shrieks of whistles pierce the quiet.

"Get up, get up, you lazy oafs, you creepy, droopy wrigglers," Bob shouts, his face a deep shade of purple and a large vein pulsing in his forehead over his left eye. He's standing beside my bed, only inches from my face. I could stick out my hand and pinch him, only I don't dare.

Mother Ma'am is on the other side of the bars. She has her hands on her hips and is glaring at the bodies still lumped into shapes of sleep on their bunks. Every few seconds she flips the light switch up and down rapidly. I rub my eyes. Most of the others are already standing beside their bunks, straight as rods, their arms held close to their sides. They're all dressed the same: in black pants and white collared shirts, and black blazers with "LB" embroidered on the pockets. They would look like waiters, or hotel bellmen, or butlers, except that most of their clothes are torn—sleeves attached to shoulders with only a few remaining stitches, pant legs sliced and frayed.

I crawl down from my bunk and stand beside Trevor. He looks just as bad as he did yesterday, except his face has lost its greenish tinge and is now a pasty gray. His clothes are rumpled from being slept in. His stomach fizzes and pops loudly, and he's rubbing circles against it with his palm.

"You sorry lot are permitted to head to the mess hall," Bob yells, when it appears that everyone is down from his or her bunk. He slides the bars back, and the men start crossing the room to join the line filing out the door on the other side. Trevor and I turn to do the same, but Mother Ma'am strides across the room and puts one hand on each of our heads, forcing us to sit on Trevor's mattress.

"You new little Uglies can stay right where you are." It's the first time I've heard her speak, and her words slide so quietly into the space between us that I have to lean forward to catch them. "You newcomers ate enough on the plane to do without breakfast today."

When everyone else is out of the building, Mother

Ma'am turns and grins at Trevor and me, and motions for us to follow her to the door, where Emily and Maggie are waiting.

"You kiddies are in for a treat," she hisses. Her yellowed teeth are sharp and jagged, and I take a step backwards. "You get to meet the Royals."

She strides out the front door and we follow behind. It's my first look at Lily Brook in the daylight. When we arrived last night it was too dark to see anything but the parking lot and the six concrete bunkhouses; now I realize that this is all there is to see. Except for a long narrow building tucked behind our bunkhouse with "Mess Hall" painted on the side, there's nothing to Lily Brook but the buildings that were visible last night.

Nothing except for this: beside the guards' house is a steel gate that seems to rise five stories into the air. The gate is attached to a large concrete wall just as tall, with a heap of twisted metal and barbed wire on the top. I pivot around. Lily Brook is no larger than a football field and this cement wall surrounds all of it.

Well, almost all of it. Behind the mess hall the gate ends for a section, revealing the edge of Poplova Forest. But it's not the lush green forest that Emily imagined while we were on the plane. And it's nothing at all like the forest in Currency, where I spent my days with Archduke Pooch. It's a bleak and gloomy forest, with knobby branches jabbing out this way and that, and spiky vines spilling in every direction. A dark forest that seems to force back all the light around it, so that while the Lily Brook parking lot is rather bright, the area near the forest is a pattern of dingy shadows.

"Get in." Mother Ma'am walks over to the closest mail truck and swings open the back.

Once we're seated on the bench she slams the door shut. The truck jerks forward and stalls a half-dozen times before the engine catches, and the sudden burst of speed sends Trevor sprawling onto the rusty floor. There's no window to look out of, and Emily doesn't even bother to imagine one this time. A loud screech shatters the silence as the gate opens, and a shuddering crash follows as it closes behind us.

"There's something sad about Mother Ma'am," Maggie says, after a moment.

"Sad?" Trevor raises his eyebrows. "As in short for sadistic? Cruel, brutal, vicious …"

"Just sad. Her lips tremble when she talks. I don't think she's happy here."

"Surprising, considering our lovely surroundings." Trevor sweeps his arm as if he's showing off a game show prize. "Luxury accommodation nestled in a beautiful gated compound. Rest your head on an authentic saw-dust pillow; cuddle up under a threadbare sheet. Pleasant dreams guaranteed when the bed you're sleeping on could collapse at any moment. Really, what's not to be happy about?"

"Yeah." Emily grins at him. "It's kind of fun, isn't it? Rustic."

"Emily, I was just …" But he stops and shakes his head.

"Did you notice it, Danny?" Maggie asks, resting her hand on my arm.

Calling Mother Ma'am sad seems deluded. Fearsome, yes. Menacing, absolutely. But I glance at Maggie's hand resting just below my elbow, her thin fingers, her chewed nails, and instead of arguing, I find myself agreeing with her.

"Maybe. A little."

WHEN MOTHER MA'AM opens the back of the truck, we step onto a bright green lawn clipped as short as the hair on Bob's head. To one side is the same dark forest that's at the edge of the compound, but on the other side is mile after mile of rolling emerald hills, and in front of us is the grandest house I have ever seen. No, it isn't a house; it's the castle from the Lily Brook brochure. In the parking lot are five other mail trucks.

Mother Ma'am marches towards the castle and we follow behind her. We walk up the gold-paved drive, flanked by magnificent sculpted bushes and vibrant flowers, to a large wooden door with a nameplate beside it. "Their Royal Highnesses, The Brook Family," the plate reads.

Mother Ma'am reaches for a button below the nameplate.

"Hello," barks a voice that seems to be coming from the wall.

"The new Uglies have arrived."

"About time." The door swings open.

Inside, the house glows. The staircase banister is studded with diamonds. The paintings on the wall are framed in gold. The ceiling is a mosaic of gemstones.

"Wow." Maggie swipes her finger along the wall. "It's beautiful."

"Neat-o." Emily reaches for a picture frame and Mother Ma'am smacks her hand away.

"It's even bigger than my houses," whispers Trevor in disbelief.

We follow Mother Ma'am through the hallway into the ballroom. The room is the size of the entire Lily Brook compound, and stacked around the perimeter are large wooden crates with thick padlocks. On one side the huge windows look out across rolling green hills, but through the windows on the other side, the dark Poplova woods leer at us.

The forest around my home is my favorite place to go, and I used to spend every free moment building forts, climbing trees, and netting fish in the creeks and streams that run into Midasville River. Sometimes, Pooch and I blazed our own paths through the brush and I'd imagine we were the first boy-and-dog team to discover Currency, and that we'd have to survive on berries and roasted squirrels until we'd cleared enough land to build a home with a garden, just for us.

When I was younger I told Father I wanted to be an explorer.

"Ridiculous," he replied. "Everything's been discovered. There's no point wasting your life doing things that have already been done by someone else." But Mother says some people have a way of looking at old things that makes them seem new; she says there are plenty of places worth exploring. I guess I had hoped that Poplovastan could be one, that when I *was* allowed to go home I could tell Father stories about the adventures I'd had and the things I'd seen, and that maybe he'd be proud of me. But Pooch isn't here and Poplova Forest doesn't really seem like a place I'd want to wander around in alone.

I'm staring at the woods through the window when a familiar orange braid snakes into view and a hand clamps my shoulder.

"Keeping us waiting, Ugly?" Captain Ma'am maneuvers me towards the far wall, where three leather sofas are arranged in front of a large fireplace. The rest of the Lily Brook newcomers are sitting in a tight line a couple of paces back. Some of them are sniffling, others are sobbing, but most of them are perfectly silent. I look for José and find him huddled at the edge of the row with his legs tucked to his chest. His pants and jacket are crumpled and streaked with dirt, and he's rubbing at the toes of his boots with a monogrammed handkerchief.

I sit beside him and whisper hello, but he stares straight ahead and doesn't answer. I follow his eyes to the sofa on the left, where three large men sit squeezed together. They are almost identical in their appearance—their brown hair hangs in a shag of bangs just above their small piggy eyes. They wear beige trousers that have been pressed so that a crease runs up the center of each leg, shiny brown shoes, and button-down shirts that pinch the skin of their fleshy necks. The man on the left in the trio has a yo-yo looped over his finger and is thrusting it up and down, up and down. The next man holds a remote control and is racing a small red car back and forth at his feet. The man leaning against the right armrest holds a bag of candies in his lap and stuffs handfuls of them into his mouth. They all look to be in their forties, but giggle and stab at one another with their elbows as though they are children.

A woman in a long black evening gown is lounging across the sofa on the far right. Her feet—strapped into silver high heels—rest on the far armrest. Her brown hair is piled on the top of her head in a mountain of stiff curls that don't move at all when she touches them. A cloud of perfume hovers in the air above her, and her face is caked with so much makeup that she looks more like a wax figure in a museum than a person.

On the sofa in the center are the only two people I recognize. They are both older now, more wrinkled, and the woman has puffed out a bit in her face and around her middle, but there is no denying that these are Mr. and Mrs. Brook, the founders of Lily Brook. His hair has faded to white and he's so thin his navy suit seems to swallow him. Beside him, his pudgy wife sits primly in a matching navy skirt suit. Every inch of skin and fabric is draped or pinned with jewelry, from the enormous diamonds in her ears to the gold chains dangling around her neck, all the way to the jeweled broaches covering her lapel. Her hair is dyed a shade of purplish brown and is permed into a halo of curls. Her gloved hands rest folded in her lap.

Compared with Captain Ma'am and the guards standing off to the side of the couches, the Brooks look positively timid. It's hard to feel threatened by men who play with toys, and the woman in the evening gown is wearing heels so high she'd probably topple over if she tried to come after any of us. Mr. and Mrs. Brook looked frightening in the brochure, but now they just look like regular old people, members of the Midasville Lawn Bowling Team or the Bake Sale Brigade. From what the rest of the Uglies said last night, I had expected the Royals to be terrifying, but they don't seem that scary at all.

Not until they open their mouths, that is.

XI

THE WOMAN IN THE EVENING GOWN is the first to break the heavy silence that fills the ballroom. "My sister Lily was a repulsive, snotty bratwurst, just like you people." She waves lazily, gesturing at the group of us seated in front of her. "We are doing your families a favor by letting them ship you here."

"And they're doing us a favor by paying a million buckaroos a year for each of you," laughs the man on the left in the trio on the couch.

"A million buckaroos and an army of little slaves." The man on the right sniggers, spewing bits of chewed-up candy at the new Lily Brook residents sitting closest to his feet.

"Silence." As soon as Mr. Brook speaks, his sons sit upright and cross their hands in their laps. I catch myself doing the same. The old man leans back in his chair and smiles widely at the group of us.

"My family and I always take a special interest in Lily Brook newcomers. We make certain that our expectations are expressed clearly, in order to avoid any misunderstandings." His voice is eight times the size of his frail body, and booms to fill the hall. The ache of hunger in my stomach skitters and twists into a thousand butterfly wings and a sharp, sour taste fills my mouth. I swallow hard.

"We do not like misunderstandings." Mr. Brook leans forward and stares from one newcomer to the next. "But we are confident that they can be avoided as long as the three principles of Lily Brook are remembered by all residents."

The room is so quiet that the sound of José rubbing his handkerchief against his boot seems to echo off the walls. He must notice this too, because he stops and wraps his arms around his knees.

"Firstly, you will obey. You will obey because you will not want to discover the consequences of disobeying." As soon as Mr. Brook says it, I turn to look at José. From the shuffling noises around me, I can tell that pretty much everybody else is looking at him too. But José doesn't seem to notice. His eyes are squeezed shut.

Mr. Brook snorts out a laugh. "Believe me, that one got off easy. Others have been much less fortunate."

"Tell them, tell them, tell them," chant the Brook brothers, bouncing in their seats.

"Let's just say that the last person who refused a Brook's demand is no longer in the position to speak about it." Mr. Brook reaches over and rests his hand on his wife's thick arm. She beams at him.

"The King," the candy-eating son shouts triumphantly. "The King refused. And Daddy told me to get out Squeeze and Gripper. Our boa constrictors!" He makes a motion with his hands as if he's strangling the neck of an invisible person perched on the arm of the couch.

"Shut up!" Mr. Brook stands and slaps his son's temple with the back of his hand. The man shrieks and covers his head with his arms. He rubs vigorous circles against the spot his father hit. Then, slowly, glancing towards Mr. Brook as he does, he moves one hand away and makes a fist—then pops his thumb into his mouth.

I rub my own head. A stabbing pain is shooting from my eyes down through my neck. I wish I had a cool cloth and some lemon water—Mother's headache remedy—but I shudder when I think of what Captain Ma'am would say if I asked.

"Secondly, you own nothing." Mr. Brook is more animated now. He walks back and forth in front of the seats his children are lounging in, punching the air with his fist as he speaks. "Everything you brought with you belongs to us: your wallets, your clothes, your suitcases." He pushes his lips into a pout and screws his fists against his eyes. "Your little-wittle teddy bears." With that, his daughter, who has been examining her fingernails, begins to giggle. "Even the lint in your pockets belongs to the Brook Family!"

"And everything you find in the forest," adds the man with the remote control car. "If you find the—"

"And everything you find is ours," Mr. Brook interrupts, glaring at his son.

I glance out the window. Whatever is in that forest I don't want coming anywhere near me. What do the Brooks think we could possibly want to keep? Pet wolves and cougars? A family of poisonous snakes? Do snakes even live in Poplovastan? I can't believe I didn't ask Brittany these things before I left. As for giving the Brooks my trunk, I have my books in there, and family pictures. I have my special pillow. I have a batch of Mother's chocolate-coconut cookies. Inside my pockets, I ball my hands into fists.

As I do, the knuckles of my right hand skim Mother's button. I won't let the Brooks take that, no matter what they threaten me with. I close my eyes and try to picture Mother, sitting on the bench in the rose garden wearing her ratty coat. Maybe at this exact moment she is touching the place the button was, and thinking about me. I imagine I can reach out my thoughts to her—*come and get me*, I repeat over and over in my head, *take me home*. But Mrs. Brook interrupts my concentration.

"You children grew up with many privileges, and it will improve your character to learn to live without them." It's the first time she has spoken. Her voice is high-pitched and flute-like, and while she talks she flutters her fingers in her lap and stares down at her lacy white gloves. "We ourselves had an unfortunate encounter with poverty once. A simply dreadful event that I need not discuss except to say this." She looks up and glares at us, her brown eyes blazing. "Many of your families were aware of our circumstances and none of them came to our assistance."

Mr. Brook pats his wife's leg, and she leans back in her seat again and refolds her hands in her lap.

"Finally." Mr. Brook clears his throat. "The third and most important principle for you to keep in mind is that at Lily Brook, residents are disposable." He sits back in his seat and smiles broadly.

Disposable? What is that supposed to mean? I glance down the row. A few kids are crying—blowing their noses into their sleeves or wiping tears from their cheeks with their hands—but most of them are sitting perfectly still, staring at Mr. Brook with wide-open mouths. José has his head tucked into his jacket, so all that's visible are a couple of drooping spikes of hair, but even they seem to be quivering.

"Your job is hard," continues Mr. Brook. "You will get injured. You will not, however, come crying to us, because we are not concerned with your well-being. The last thing the King told us before he handed over the deed to half his country was that there have been many deaths in Poplova Forest. I'd have been worried, but I have no need to go near the place. That is *your* job."

"In the forest," pipes up the Brook with the yo-yo, "there are vines that can slice you in half!" He raises his arm, then chops his brother's knee with the side of his hand. The chopped Brook throws his remote control at his brother's face, then shoves him so hard he falls off the couch. The candy-eating brother flops himself on top of the fallen Brook son and begins to pummel him with his fists.

"And there are branches that can strangle the life out of you." The Brook daughter yawns and stretches her arms over her head.

The room is silent. We have all turned to stare out the large windows.

"You'll get a better look at it up close this afternoon." Mr. Brook turns to Captain Ma'am. "You may take them away, Elmira." With that he leaves the room, ushering his wife and children in front of him.

When they have gone, Captain Ma'am stands and claps her hands, and immediately we all form a line and follow her out of the castle to the row of mail trucks. I climb into Mother Ma'am's truck quickly, to avoid being thrown inside by one of the guards, who are pulling the stragglers across the lot by their ears. On our way to the compound, Trevor starts his game show routine again.

"And if the luxurious accommodation at Lily Brook isn't enough for you, consider taking a moonlit stroll in Poplova Forest. If you manage to survive the strangling vines and slicing branches, you'll have enough stories to entertain your friends and neighbors for a lifetime. And if you don't survive, you'll save on airfare for the return trip."

"Do you suppose they're really serious about the forest?" I ask, although I'm already quite certain they are.

"I'll bet hundreds of scientists would love to have a look at Poplova Forest, study it, you know, but only we've got the chance." Emily grins.

"Shut up, Dopey." It's José. I didn't even see him get in. He's huddled at the back of the truck, shaking.

"What did she do to you?" Maggie asks.

He stares at her and shakes his head, then turns away from us. No one says anything for the rest of the short ride back. Even Emily has started to look a little green.

XII

THE TRUCKS PULL INTO THE LOT and we are all herded to a shed beside the mess hall. Inside are heaping piles of black pants, white shirts, and black blazers with "LB" embroidered in gold above the pockets. Most are threadbare and all are stained with food, mud, and streaks of something that looks like blood.

"Find a uniform that fits and get into the hall to change. Girls first, boys second. Leave your old clothes in the garbage can by the counter. If you have anything," Captain Ma'am glares at us, "and I mean *anything*, in your pockets, put it in the box beside the garbage can now. You will see that it is much preferable to part with your treasures at this point than to risk me finding them at some later date."

I feel for the button in my pocket. *It's just a button*, I tell myself. *She'd hardly care about one little button. And how would she even find it?* But José is beside me shivering, so it's hard to kid myself. *She would do to you what she did to him*, I answer myself back. *Or worse*.

"These uniforms are designed to make you look like servants." Captain Ma'am is holding one of the jackets up, pinched between her thumb and forefinger. "To boost morale." She pauses, then snickers. "In fact, most of the guards agree that seeing you all dressed like this boosts their morale quite a bit."

I find a pair of pants that will fit me if I roll the cuffs up a turn or two, and a shirt that is a little snug, but satisfactory. The suit jackets are all much too big, and I can just imagine what Father would say about the fit.

Thinking about Father makes a lump swell in my throat again. I close my eyes and wonder what my family is doing this very instant—Father would be meeting with his financial advisors in his study or shouting at them over the telephone. My sisters are back at Midas Millions. Mother is probably in the garden or reading a book by the bay window in the front room—or perhaps she's standing beside the mantel, with our family photograph pressed to her chest, missing me. I wonder if she's written me a letter yet, like she promised. I wonder when I'll see her next, and if she'll come and take me away from this place because she can't bear to be without me. But Captain Ma'am said that no one has ever written a letter to a Lily Brook resident, no one has even tried to visit here. Maybe

Mother won't miss me at all. In fact, maybe she's already forgotten that I exist.

Captain Ma'am's loud bark interrupts my thoughts. "And if I find out you've smuggled so much as a stick of bubble gum into your pockets, you'll get a wallop that will send you halfway through to next week." She lowers her voice and winks at José. "Or maybe something worse than that."

———— ✺ ————

I CLUTCH THE BUTTON in my fist when I go inside to change, then pretend to bend down and scratch my ankle, pushing it into my sock. One of the guards is watching me, but he turns and shouts something at a scrawny kid near the doorway, then marches away. Beside me, a boy sticks a photograph of a dog into his shoe.

When I go to the garbage can to throw out my old clothes, the box beside it is already full of coins, Swiss Army knives, house keys, and tubes of lip-gloss. There are a handful of fuzz-coated cough drops on the top of the pile, and it takes some restraint to stop from reaching in and sticking the lot of them in my mouth. I haven't eaten anything since the stale cupcakes on the airplane and I'm starting to feel dizzy. Trevor sees me hovering.

"You hungry, Danny?"

In answer to his question, my stomach lets out a loud growl.

"Here," he says, holding out a small metal box. It's filled with a nest of dark maroon threads.

"What's that?"

"Kashmiri Mongra saffron. Harvested recently too." He prods the strands with his finger. "Notice the moistness, the elasticity? You do know what saffron is, don't you?" he asks, when I don't answer. "From the saffron crocus?"

"A spice?" I offer. "You can't eat spices by themselves, can you?"

Trevor shrugs. "What a waste if I don't. You know how difficult this stuff is to get?" He offers me the box again, but I shake my head.

"Suit yourself." He dumps the contents into his mouth and grins, but almost as quickly as his smile appears it vanishes, and he is grabbing for the edge of the garbage can, choking and sputtering until a weasel-faced guard offers to teach him a lesson about making too much noise.

"Intense," he whispers to me, once he manages to regain composure. "Don't try *that* at home."

⤙⤚

WHEN WE'RE ALL DRESSED and standing in a row beside the shed, Captain Ma'am throws open the back door of the mess hall. "Which of you web-toed weasels would like to be on lunch bucket duty?"

Beside me, Emily shoots up her hand.

"Nice to see Miss Knob Knees volunteering herself and the rest of the Uglies."

José glares at Emily.

"Er, sorry, José ... I didn't mean ..."

"Save it."

We step into the kitchen, where four uniformed guards are stirring pots over four large stoves. There's a white plastic bucket on the floor—the size of a small child's swimming pool. I could likely sit against one side and stretch my toes out to touch the other. One by one the guards pour their pots into the bucket.

"Okay, then," snaps Captain Ma'am, when the last pot has been emptied. "You may carry that to the parking lot."

"But …" says Trevor.

"But …" mimics Captain Ma'am. "But we're too wimpy, too flimsy, too whiny. Suck it up, you ungrateful little upchuck, or you and the rest of the Uglies can wait until tomorrow to eat."

Captain Ma'am leaves us standing in a circle around the bucket. The four guards take off their aprons and wipe their foreheads, then lean against the stoves and watch. Trevor's eyes wander around the kitchen.

"This place is hardly up to code," he whispers to me. "And it smells worse than the Biggo Burger test kitchen. Sauerkraut," he says, sniffing the air. "Also lima beans and maybe beef chuck."

Emily interrupts him. "If we space ourselves evenly and each grab part of the rim, we should be able to lift it."

"I've about had it with you and your bright ideas." José grabs the part of the rim closest to him and gives it a strong tug. The bucket doesn't move an inch, but the liquid inside, a frothy brown mixture with hunks of something floating near the surface, starts to swirl in the center and then forms a wave that races to the edge of the bucket and splashes onto him.

"Yeow!" He is drenched from the middle of his chest to below his knees. "I'm burned! I'm filthy!" A few pieces of something solid have landed on his uniform, and Trevor leans over and picks one off, then pops it into his mouth. He grimaces.

"No seasoning whatsoever."

"Get your grubby hands off me." José steps away from us and begins flicking the soup chunks from his blazer. We wait a moment for him to finish, but it seems he has no intention of helping us. Trevor, Maggie, Emily, and I each grab part of the rim and hoist the bucket ourselves, as high as we can manage, until the bottom is just barely skimming the ground. José walks behind us, wringing out his shirt and muttering under his breath. The liquid in the bucket swirls and sloshes with every step. By the time we reach Captain Ma'am, standing beside the last mail truck, tapping her foot and shaking her head, the four of us are as wet as José, if not wetter.

"Hurry up, you slobbering sloths," Captain Ma'am barks. But as hard as we try, we can't lift the bucket high enough to get it into the truck. Captain Ma'am takes a step towards José, and as soon as she does he stops muttering and rushes to help us. On Emily's count of three, we heave the bucket with all our might until the corner is perched on the lip of the truck, then we shove it hard and crawl in after it, huffing and puffing and panting for breath.

We drive for twenty, maybe thirty, minutes before the truck lurches to a stop, sending a splatter of congealing brown liquid in every direction.

"Out!" Captain Ma'am throws open the back door. The sky is dark, though it can't be nighttime yet. And the air is heavy with noise: rustling, panting, sharp thwacks of metal against wood.

Our mail truck is last in a chain of about twenty others. On one side of the trucks—where the guards are lounging—is a grassy meadow speckled with wildflowers, but even without the guards to spoil the view the field hardly looks inviting. From across the road, the trees throw sinister shadows on the grass, shadows that dispel all light from around them, turning the meadow a dingy gray.

Captain Ma'am shoves us in the other direction, towards a strip of dirt and fallen logs, a few piles of twisted branches, and—beyond that—a line of trees that form a wall that seems impenetrable: Poplova Forest. Swinging axes and machetes at the vines and branches twisted around them are all of our fellow Lily Brook residents.

XIII

THE FOREST HERE is even darker than it appeared to be at the compound, even bleaker and more menacing. And what's worse is that the Brooks' horror stories weren't exaggerations. The forest is doing something that seems impossible; the forest is moving.

It isn't just that the branches are swaying in the wind; they're hurtling towards the line of Lily Brookers at the forest edge—aiming for their chests, and stomachs and eyes. The vines swing fast as whips to knock axes from hands. They lash at arms or creep slowly along the forest floor and wrap themselves around ankles.

"Lunchtime," one of the guards calls, and the other residents rush to line up at the back of Captain Ma'am's mail truck, throwing their equipment in a heap by the door. From their pockets they each pull a rusted tin can. A couple of guards drag the giant bucket so that it's hanging halfway out the rear doors of the truck, and one by one the residents dip their cans into it, then sit down on the ground at the edge of the forest and drink.

I smell something incredible, but it can't be coming from the bucket. I was sitting next to it for the whole ride out and it made me more nauseous than hungry. Then I notice the guards hovering near the front door of one of the other mail trucks. They're pulling food from paper bags: foil pouches stuffed with chicken wings, large slices of iced chocolate cake, hunks of buttered bread, baggies of sliced vegetables. They shove the food into their mouths by the handful.

José, Trevor, Maggie, Emily, and I join the end of the lunch line. Captain Ma'am thrusts a battered metal can into each of our hands. When we reach the bucket, there's only a thin layer of liquid left at the bottom. José scrapes his can through it but it comes out empty. He glares at Emily and throws his can to the ground.

"Here." Emily kneels down and flips his can so it's upright, then shoves in front of him and pulls the bucket to rest on her knees. She tips it into José's can.

"You next, Danny." I step forward and let Emily pour a stream of liquid into my can. She fills Trevor's and Maggie's too, so all that is left for her is a final trickle.

"I'm still full from the cupcakes, really," she shrugs.

"Hey, thanks," Trevor, Maggie, and I say at once.

José picks up his can the ground and brushes the dirt from the side, then goes over to a rock near the edge of the forest and slumps down with his back towards us.

We join Uncle Ernst and some of the other Uglies I recognize from the morning procession through the dorm. They're sitting on a mound of sawdust.

"What *is* this?" I take a sip from the can and force myself to swallow. It tastes like dishwater—salty and soapy and a little bit bitter.

"Same as every lunch." Uncle Ernst scrapes the last bit of liquid from his can with his fingers and then sticks them in his mouth. "Supper soup."

"What's supper soup?" Even though Trevor made gagging sounds when the liquid first touched his lips, he drank his entire can of soup before we'd reached the other Uglies and now he's eyeing mine.

"They take what's left over from supper," a small pear-shaped woman beside Uncle Ernst explains. "Put it into a couple of pots and add enough water so that it'll fill the bucket once it's heated through."

"That's disgusting." José has wandered over and is standing behind us.

"Sometimes it's disgusting," Uncle Ernst shrugs. "Today it's sauerkraut and lima beans and some sort of mystery meat. Not my favorite, but hardly disgusting compared with what it has been."

Just then a whistle blows.

"Back to work." Uncle Ernst shoves his can into his pocket. The others in the group follow suit. I drain the last of my supper soup into my mouth and jump up to join the rest of the Lily Brookers, who are grabbing tools from the pile near the truck. Maggie and I each pick up small knives not much sharper than butter knives and step towards the vines at the edge of the forest.

I turn to the woman beside us. She has smooth dark skin and white hair cropped close to her head. She isn't looking at her machete, but, even so, the blade finds the vines in front of her. She seems as comfortable with the weapon as Brittany is with her dissecting scalpel or Annabelle with her mirror.

"What do I do?"

"Just cut," she yells as a vine swings towards me. She lunges for it, slicing the center with her machete. The vine falls to the ground, twisting and flopping, before it shrivels into a knot at her feet. When I look up, another vine is hurtling towards us. I hold out my knife and tighten my grip, but the vine hits the blade hard and knocks me, stumbling, backwards. I reach out to steady myself and catch the branch of a tree. It's as if I were holding shattered glass.

"Ow!" I pull my hand off and fall to the ground. My palm is bloody and shards of tree bark are sticking out of my skin.

A hand clamps down on my shoulder.

"You looking to take a nap, Ugly?" One of the guards is glaring over me. I hold up my hand to show her why I've fallen. "You expect to get sympathy because of that, do you? Believe me, I've seen that forest dish out much,

much worse." She grabs the collar of my shirt and yanks me up.

"Are you okay?" Maggie whispers, once the guard leaves.

"Fine," I say, but my eyes are blurred and it looks as though there are two Maggies standing there with their hands in their jacket pockets, vines looming behind them.

"Look out!" I scream. But Maggie doesn't move, and only at the last minute does an oncoming vine arc away. "Where's your knife?"

"That seems awfully mean, don't you think? Cutting them." She's staring into the forest with her head cocked to one side. I see the glint of a knife blade in the dirt at her feet.

"They're just vines, Maggie. It's not like they can feel it."

"They're not ordinary vines, though," she says. Another one whips towards her, and I leap to slice it away.

"And maybe they can't feel the knives," she gazes at the sliced vine, as it flops on the ground between us. "But what if they can?"

I kick the now-shriveled vine towards the trees. Maggie's right about one thing: these are not ordinary vines. But even if they can feel our knives, that's no reason not to cut them. Either we chop the vines, or they slash us. And when I do get a chance to leave Lily Brook, I want it to be in one piece.

THE SUN HAS STARTED TO SET before we are allowed to board the trucks and go back to the compound. Maggie and I pile into a truck with a group of twenty or so others, Emily and José among them. My body aches and my clothes are ripped and dirty. I have cuts and lashes on my arms and face. My shins are bruised from swinging tree branches that I wasn't quick enough to leap over. Emily's as filthy as I am, but José's uniform—although dirty and rumpled—looks no dirtier and no more rumpled than it did when we arrived.

"Did you even get near the forest?" I ask him.

"You should have seen it," Emily answers, before José has a chance to respond. "Every time a vine sliced towards him, he leaped over it, or twirled away from it. He pirouetted."

"I did *not* pirouette," José says in a low growl.

"But you did! Pirouettes, chassés, échappés, jetés." Emily flips her hands around, demonstrating. "My mom enrolled me in ballet for years, and I was awful at it. I'm not exactly graceful. But you …"

"Shut up," José snarls and pushes his way to a spot on the other side of the mail truck.

"What's wrong?" Emily calls after him, but José doesn't turn around. She stares at his back for a long moment. "What did I say?"

"Maybe he's just tired." Maggie pats Emily's arm.

"But, what …" Emily continues, but the truck engine rumbles and her words are drowned out. Before long we're lurching and bumping along. No one speaks much. I close my eyes and am almost asleep when someone clears his throat.

"Hey, Ernst?"

There's no reply. Uncle Ernst must be on another truck.

"So, new kids." It's the throat-clearer speaking. "Anyone ever tell you what happened to Miss Lily Brook?"

"She died." I can still see her smiling picture on the back of the brochure. "She was in an air balloon with her family but she jumped out and killed herself."

Someone starts to laugh.

"She did." I feel my cheeks flush hot. "It was in the brochure."

"The brochure always says *that*, but do you know what really happened to her?" This voice, deep and slow, comes from beside me.

"She was pushed." From behind me.

"No, kicked." Softly from somewhere near my feet.

"She was lifted up and dropped." A husky voice to my right.

"Regardless," says the first voice. "The Brooks killed her."

"And they were caught," replies the soft voice. "Someone saw them in the act. Some Hawaiian families. A whole group of them."

"And they went to the press," adds someone else. "And pretty soon it was all over the news."

"I remember that," sighs someone. "I was just a kid, but I remember that."

"And then," continues the first voice, "Mr. Remroddinger wrote a suicide note and planted it in a locket near the side of the volcano."

I don't say anything. I wish with all my might that they're just trying to scare us. That pretty soon everyone will start laughing and tell us that they made it all up. But there is silence. A few long minutes go by.

"Is that all really true?" I finally ask.

No one answers, but they don't need to. I am sure that it is.

XIV

THE TRUCKS DRIVE US BACK to the lot by the dorms and from there we walk to the mess hall. Four guards are already standing at the far end of the room with a stack of plates beside them and three large barrels of food at their feet. "Menu," is scrawled on a chalkboard by the entrance door. "Chicken skin, boiled onions, soybean mush."

"That might just make a nice supper soup tomorrow." I turn to see if the woman beside me is joking, but a smile has crept onto her face and she is licking her lips.

The food is horrible, but getting attacked by trees really helps a person build up an appetite, and when I'm finished I bend my face to my plate and lick off every last splatter of grease and onion juice. Only the guards have cutlery.

I'm at a table with a bunch of other Uglies, and when José slumps in beside me with his plate, Emily immediately grabs his arm.

"I'm just wondering something."

He shakes her off and spreads out a rubbery piece of chicken skin on his plate without acknowledging her.

"You're obviously extremely accomplished at ballet, and I'm just curious why you're here, when this place is supposedly for ordinary people."

José continues arranging his food, placing his soybeans and onions on the chicken skin, and wrapping them up like a burrito. He doesn't respond to Emily, but his ears are red.

"You're a ballerina?" Trevor raises his eyebrows. "Like with a tutu?"

"I don't know what you're talking about," José glares at Emily. He takes a bite of his chicken skin burrito, and while he chews it his faces flushes pinker and pinker until it's a deep crimson. "But the correct term for a male ballet dancer," he mutters, "is *danseur*."

"How do you know th …" But when José turns towards him, the words seem to dry up on Trevor's tongue. We eat the rest of our dinner in silence.

AFTER DINNER, the guards march us back to the dorms. Uncle Ernst shows us the washhouse out back, beside the row of outhouses, and he and I stand side by side and scrub at our shirts to loosen some of the dirt from the fabric.

I watch Ernst's hands as he works. The action seems automatic—he scrubs, rinses, then wrings out the fabric, scrubs, rinses, wrings it out again. He must have done the same thing every evening for the last twenty years.

"Have you been cutting the forest every day, the whole time you've been here?" I ask.

"Yes." Ernst takes a step away from the sink and twists his shirt over the ground, then shakes the creases from the fabric. He doesn't look at me.

"And are you any closer to the mountain? Has there ever been a tree that didn't grow back the second it was cut?"

"No, Danny."

"So why are we cutting them? If the Brooks want us for slaves you'd think we could do something a little more useful."

Ernst doesn't say anything, and I turn back to the sink and start to pick at a mud stain with my fingernail. But then I remember what one of the Brooks' sons said: *Anything you find in the forest is ours.*

"There's something in the forest, isn't there? Something the Brooks want?"

Ernst nods, then steps towards me and takes my left hand—the one not cut up by shards of bark—and folds it into a fist, motioning for me to scrub at the stains with my knuckles.

I pull away. "What? What's in there?"

"There's a well." Ernst steps closers and begins to wash my shirt himself.

"A well?" It doesn't make sense. Is there not enough water in Poplovastan? Even if there isn't a lake, like the brochure claimed, surely the Brooks are rich enough to fly their water in.

"Some say a special sort of well."

"What sort?" What sort of well could be worth all this?

"A wishing well."

"A wishing well?" It's the closest I've come to laughing since I first heard about Lily Brook. "The Brooks believe in *wishing* wells?"

Ernst ignores me. He pulls up a block of wood and sits down. "When I first came to Lily Brook, I had a great friend, Bruno. He and I got along right away. We both considered ourselves chess masters, and he had smuggled a knife back into the dorm and carved game pieces from a few sticks. We used to play at night behind the washbasins. Bruno was funny, and smart, and tough too. He always stood beside me when we were cutting at the forest, beating back any vines that came towards the two of us. I was scrawny then, and very little help.

"Bruno had a kid brother who was some kind of chemistry whiz and he had subscriptions to every science journal you could think of. One journal had run an article about Poplovastan at some point, and Bruno ripped it out and brought it with him. He read it to us."

As Ernst talks about his old friend, I can't stop thinking about the Brooks. "But they can't really believe in wishing wells, can they?"

Ernst doesn't answer me, but continues on with his story.

"It was years ago that Bruno left, but I still remember most of what the article said. The well is in a cave at the base of Mount Poplova, and was dug just over a century ago. The water has special properties—the result of a magic spell—and can grant wishes to those who drink it. Poplova Forest acts as the well's guardian. Of course, these are legends that the villagers tell. The only thing the article said for certain was that sometime after Poplova's last volcanic activity the forest surrounding the mountain went through a number of physical changes, and most of the wildlife disappeared."

"But you believe the well is magic."

"The Brooks do, I suppose. For the rest of us, the forest is just the way we spend our days."

"The way you spend your days?" I repeat. "Just the way you spend your days!" I say again, my voice rising. But Ernst doesn't seem to share my frustration at all. He shrugs his shoulders.

I turn back to the sink and start cleaning the scratches on my arms and face. The Brooks have us fighting the forest every day because of a fairy tale, and even worse than that: no one seems to care. Ernst certainly isn't acting too upset. He's whistling under his breath as he wrings out my shirt. I'm so busy being angry that I rub my hands together under the faucet, driving the bark deeper into my right palm.

"Ouch!" When I start picking at the slivers still wedged

deep inside my skin, I only manage to slice my palm up more.

"Let me see that." Ernst takes my hand. He gently plucks at the bark with the tips of his fingernails and flicks the pieces to the ground. With every shiver of pain the whole situation seems worse and worse. And then I think about what Ernst said. *It was years ago that Bruno left.*

"Ernst?"

"L.B. Caruthers," Ernst says.

"What?"

"L.B. Caruthers was the scientist who wrote the article. I can't believe I still remember that. A volcano expert, I think."

"Did Bruno get to go home?"

Ernst pulls the last sliver from my hand. "Good as new."

"Did he?"

Uncle Ernst doesn't answer, just pats the board he's sitting on, motioning for me to join him. "Don't you try to cut too fast or too much, hear me?"

I look at him blankly.

"Every so often some newcomer gets the idea to start cutting quicker to reach the well. Some have made it deeper into the forest, but none of those folks ever made it back to Lily Brook. That's one of the reasons there are only eighty-three Uglies and not a hundred. Step into the mouth of the forest and it will swallow you, Danny Boy." With that he drops my hand, stands, and starts towards the dorm.

I sit there, staring at my swollen palm, thinking about the only other person who ever called me Danny Boy. She is so far away from me, half the world in fact. On the plane I had tried to count the days until I graduated from Lily Brook Academy. It seemed like an eternity. But there isn't a Lily Brook Academy, and I'm not going to graduate. I'm going to spend the rest of my life in Lily Brook. I will grow old here, just like Uncle Ernst is growing old. Thinking about it makes my stomach flip over. I rub at my eyes, which are blurry with tears although I hadn't realized I was crying, and follow Uncle Ernst inside. Most of the Uglies are already asleep in their beds. I lie down on mine, so tired that even the sawdust pillow feels comfortable. I close my eyes, and before I have a chance to think another thought I am asleep.

XV

UNCLE ERNST WAS RIGHT; after a while the forest becomes nothing more to me than just the way we spend our days. The first week, every day when I came back to the compound I was bruised and bloody, swollen and sore, but after a while I learned how to hold my knife into the path of the vines. I learned not to fight them but to just stand and let them come at me. By the second week some of my cuts had started to scab over and I was no longer aching at the end of every day.

Which is not to say that I'm warming up to Lily Brook. The food is terrible, the work is difficult and pointless, the guards are cruel, and the bunks are hard. But the truth is that I hardly think about any of those things because I hardly have a moment to think about them. I am either thinking about the vines coming towards me, or thinking about ways to get more supper soup into my tin can or more food onto my plate at breakfast or dinner, or I'm asleep and not thinking about anything at all—too tired to even dream. Or I'm thinking about my family. I miss Pooch, and Annabelle, Brittany, and Caroline. I miss my father. And of course I miss Mother most of all. I try to imagine what time it is in Currency, and what she might be doing. I still like to think she might be writing me letters, although none have arrived.

But even though I miss my family, I'm not lonely. I spend my days surrounded by other Lily Brookers: at meals, while we chop away at Poplova Forest, even at night in bed. And for the first time in my life, I feel like I'm making friends.

I try to stick with Maggie when we're at the forest. She's still certain that the vines can feel our knives and machetes and refuses to use one. It's not so much that I'm afraid she'll get hit by the trees—for some reason, none of them ever swing towards her—but I am afraid of what the guards might do if they notice her just standing there, and shove my own knife into her hands whenever they march by.

Trevor always knows what dinner will be as soon as we step out of the mail trucks each evening, just from the smell. And while we eat he lists different combinations of spices and seasonings that would improve the taste. For the most part, José avoids us and spends most of his time alone. Twice I've gone to the washhouse at night and spotted him leaping and twirling in the shadows at the edge of the building. Emily's right; he is a good dancer, but I've never mentioned it to him. He hasn't spoken to her since she brought it up the first time, and considering how close his bunk is to mine, I don't want to make him angry.

Finally, there's Emily, and it's hard to be too miserable around her. Her cheerfulness—though not exactly contagious—is at least distracting, and by the time she's finished rambling on about the bright side of every situation, the worst has usually passed.

THIS AFTERNOON, as Emily is talking about the best aspects of forest chopping—among them: fresh air, exercise, good company—a particularly nasty vine strikes a group of Dimwits and sends them sprawling onto the ground. They lie heaped together, moaning, except for one small boy who limp-runs for his shoe, which has shot through the air and landed beside one of the mail trucks.

"Oh no," I whisper under my breath. He's the boy I saw hiding the dog photograph beneath his insole.

I watch something flutter in the air and land on the fried chicken leg in Mother Ma'am's hand. She picks it up, smiles her sharp yellowy smile, and strides over to the truck where Captain Ma'am is napping, her stockinged feet up on the dashboard. She taps on the window, and when Captain Ma'am rolls it down, Mother

Ma'am leans in and whispers something into her ear.

Captain Ma'am throws open her door and grabs the photograph out of Mother Ma'am's hand. She thrusts her feet back into her boots, yanks them up her legs, and marches towards the boy, now on his hands and knees beside one of the mail trucks, feeling around in the dirt.

"Looking for this?" Captain Ma'am holds the photo up to his face.

He turns pale, and gulps, yet still his hand shoots out to reach for it. Captain Ma'am grabs it away as soon as his fingers get close and rips the picture in half, and then in half again, throwing the pieces on the ground. The boy starts to whimper.

Beside me a few of the Twits are whispering to one another.

"The poor dear."

"Do you suppose she'll send him to you-know-where? Or will this be punishment enough?"

"Of course she'll send him. Just you wait. Off to the dungeon with him."

"Let's hope the ghost will be quiet tonight, won't scare the boy too badly," mutters a tall woman with a round, freckled face.

"Has the ghost ever been quiet? Has the ghost ever not scared someone too badly?" The man beside her shudders. "I pity that child, that's for certain."

I step closer to them, and so do a couple of young Twits.

"Ghost?" One of them whispers to me. "Dungeon?"

I shudder and lean forward, trying to hear more details, but the older Twits have turned away and are watching Captain Ma'am yank the boy by his ear. Just before she pulls him upright, his hand reaches out, grabs a piece of the photograph, and thrusts it into the pocket of his blazer.

"He'll be getting rid of that the second he sees what he's in for," whispers one of the women, as the boy is tossed into the nearest mail truck.

When Captain Ma'am starts the truck and heads down the road, everyone watches. I listen to whispers of "dungeon" and "ghost" float between groups of older Lily Brookers. *What ghost?* I wonder. And then I remember one of the Brook brothers talking about boa constrictors and the King of Poplovastan, and the strangling motions he had made with his hands.

I walk towards José, who is sitting on a fallen log, scraping mud off his shoes with his fingernails.

"On our first night, did Captain Ma'am take you to a dungeon with a ghost?"

When José looks up at me, his face is paler than Mother Ma'am's, so white it is almost blue, and his chin is quivering. "Leave me alone, Danny."

DURING MY FIRST MONTH at Lily Brook, the trip to the dungeon for the Dimwit boy with the dog photograph is the only break from routine. We wake each morning and stand at attention beside our bunks until we're allowed to head to the mess hall for grits and watered-down coffee. After breakfast we pile into the mail trucks and are driven to the forest. We fight the vines and branches all day, with a short interruption for lunch, and when darkness falls we pile back into the trucks, are driven to the compound, eat dinner, and go to bed.

Sometimes when we're working in the forest or standing at the sinks outside the dorm, a roar starts in the sky above us and the sleek belly of Mr. Remroddinger's airplane passes over our heads, blowing cold gusts of air through the threadbare sleeves of our Lily Brook blazers. He never comes to see us, though, nor have we ever been taken to visit the Royals again. It's the guards who provide us with food and new stained clothes when ours are ripped beyond repair, who drive us to and from the forest, and who lock us into our dorms at night.

Captain Ma'am only speaks to bark orders, and spends most of her time near us clenching her strong, calloused hands into fists and cracking her knuckles. Often, when we work in the forest or sit down in the mess hall for meals, she paces among us, her thick orange braid swinging back and forth like a pendulum against her back.

Bob screams to wake us up, screams to permit us entry into the mess hall, screams to get us into the trucks, and screams wishes for nightmares at us as he locks our dorm door at night. His face is a permanent shade of scarlet, and the veins in his forehead are constantly popping out, like they're about to burst.

Every day Mother Ma'am seems even paler and thinner than the day before. She barely speaks, but instead stands behind Bob trying to look menacing. Sometimes she does, and I get chills down the back of my neck after a glance at her sharp teeth and the slits of her icy blue eyes, but other times she doesn't really look scary at all. In fact, I actually agree with Maggie: she looks a little sad.

IT IS DURING OUR SECOND MONTH at Lily Brook that there's a change. The weather gets colder and the days get shorter. Poplovastan skips from summer to winter seemingly without any warning. One morning I wake up to find ice crystals on my sawdust pillow. The air inside the dorm is so cold that I can see clouds hovering over each sleeper's mouth. Outside it's even worse. The trucks take forever to start, and halfway to the forest the one we're in plows into a snowdrift. We have to get out and push the thing free, a feat made even more difficult by the fact that two of the largest guards are seated up front and refuse to get out to help.

"The way this day is going, it'll be one for the record books," Trevor mutters, as the mail truck's spinning tires spray slush the length of his pant leg. "Absolute worst day ever."

But worse days are coming.

XVI

THE WORST DAY AT LILY BROOK starts just like any other. We wake and go to the mess hall for breakfast, scoop the grits from our plates with our fingers, and then board the mail trucks and head for the forest. When we arrive we form our usual line at the forest edge, wielding knives and axes, machetes, and sharp sticks. We're there less than an hour when a kid a few feet away from me stamps his feet and throws his ax to the ground. It's a boy with curly hair and freckles, who I've noticed always seems to duck behind his friends whenever any particularly nasty vines swing out from the forest, letting them take the brunt of the injuries. He's one of the Twits.

"This is ridiculous!" he screams.

There is quiet. Even the branches rustle less than usual. The vines begin to swing slowly, almost lazily towards us, giving us plenty of time to step away. Though none of us dare drop our tools, we're all chopping at the trees half as hard and half as often, trying to sneak peeks at the boy over our shoulders.

"This is utterly stupid!"

The guards open the front doors of their mail trucks and peer out. The gusts of warm air from the heaters form a fog cloud around them.

"Don't you agree?" The boy whirls from side to side staring at those closest to him. "Doesn't everyone agree that this is futile, that this is pointless, that this is insane?" There is dead silence. The rustling has stopped completely and the vines hang still. It's as if they are also listening to see what will happen next.

Bob has come out of his mail truck and is huddled with a group of guards near a pile of rusted machetes. "We can always count on at least one brave newcomer a year to provide us with entertainment," he says, and the rest of the guards howl with laughter.

Then a voice close to me pipes up. "I agree."

The voice belongs to José. The boy with the curly hair beams at him.

"Double the entertainment!" hoots another guard.

"Don't you agree," says the boy, more animated now, "that we'll never reach that stupid well?" He starts walking towards José. José is nodding.

"And that someone with a little guts should just go into that forest, grab a cup of that foul water, and wish themselves out of this nightmare?" José is still nodding.

I take a small step sideways and elbow him in the stomach. "No," I whisper.

"Are you with me?" The boy is beside us now. He has seized José's arm and is shaking it wildly up and down. His cheeks are flushed with excitement. José just nods.

"Is anyone else with me?" The boy turns away from José, and looks from one Lily Brooker to the next. Emily has stopped working and is staring at José with her mouth hanging open, but everyone else is still swinging their axes and machetes. The guards are quiet, watching, but most of them have their sharp teeth bared in smiles.

"Fine." The boy heads for the tool pile. "Fine. More stinking water for the two of us." He picks up two axes and crosses them over his chest.

"Don't do it!" I clutch José's collar but he twists away, leaving me with a scrap of worn fabric gripped in my fist. Emily rushes over to us.

"You can't go in there, José, it's dangerous."

"Leave me alone," he hisses, as he dodges past her.

"But it's not safe, José. You could get hurt. The trees could—"

"Get away from me, Emily. I'd rather get clobbered by trees than spend another minute in Lily Brook with you."

For a second Emily stops talking and bites her lip, but she regains her composure quickly. "But they could stab you, José. The vines could strangle you to death."

José pushes past her and grabs the machete she let drop to the ground. "Considering the alternatives, I'll take my chances."

The boy screams a blood-curdling scream and charges into the forest. José follows.

And the trees part for them.

"The trees are letting them in!" Uncle Ernst has his back turned to the forest, and I grab his arm to force him to look. "They're actually letting them in."

Uncle Ernst nods. The smile that he always wears has fallen into a loose droop and his eyes are dull.

José and the boy make it five steps into the forest, ten steps, fifteen steps, twenty. The trees and vines lean away from them. There's a clear path from the edge of the forest to the boys. Then suddenly a loud rumble starts near the mountain, and grows and grows and spreads and spreads until all the trees are shaking wildly. José has turned to stare back at us—a look of panic on his face. He takes a step towards the forest edge, but a tree to his left bends down and strikes his head with one of its branches, and then another does the same. He leaps away, performs one perfect pirouette, avoiding an onslaught of pounding branches, but then a sharp pine bough leans over to strike him in the stomach. The last I see of José, he has fallen to the forest floor, howling.

"Help me," he cries. But there's nothing that anyone can do. The vines snake over the path into the forest as soon as he speaks, coiling and twisting together. The trees shake harder and harder until even the ground at the forest edge becomes unsteady, throwing a few Lily Brookers off their feet. Then all the trees seem to arch towards José and the boy until we can no longer see them. After a moment there is silence.

"José!" Emily races along the edge of the forest, looking for a break in the trees. "José!" Maggie and I jog after her, and so do Trevor and some of the first years in the other groups. But none of the older Lily Brookers move. They stand where they are and shake their heads. A couple of them dab tears from their eyes.

Half the guards are still in hysterics—mimicking José's look of panic, the way he fell in a crumpled heap on the ground, but Bob climbs onto a stump and starts to bellow at us: "Back to work, you lazy layabouts. Chop, chop, chop. For every minute you waste with your bellyaching, you'll spend an extra hour in the forest, you'll be served one less sardine head for supper, you'll get another handful of rusty nails hammered through your bunks, you'll spend a night in the dungeon, you'll …"

Most of us face the forest and start swinging again, but Emily throws herself to the ground. "Oh, my goodness." She pounds her fists against a stump, sobbing. "It's all my fault. If he didn't hate being in my group so much …"

"It's not your fault, Emily." Maggie takes Emily's arm with one hand, lifting her to her feet. "Shush, Emily. It's okay, it'll be okay."

I hand Emily the scrap of José's collar and she wipes

her face with it and shoves it into the pocket of her blazer. Then she looks up fiercely.

"It's not okay. It won't *be* okay until I rescue him. And I will," she adds. "You can count on that."

XVII

THE NIGHT AFTER JOSÉ DISAPPEARS into the forest, I have almost fallen asleep when I hear someone tapping the bars on the other side of the curtain.

"Danny, Trevor, wake up!" I roll over and open my eyes to see Trevor already heading towards the curtain. He lifts it and ducks underneath and I follow.

"Hmm," I mumble. "What?"

"Do either of you have a plan for finding José?" I can just make out the outline of Emily's head, with her two sticking-out pigtails, on the other side of the bars. Maggie is beside her, wearing an enormous Lily Brook shirt as a nightgown.

"A plan?" I repeat, incredulous. "A plan for finding

José? In the forest? You mean going in there?"

She nods. "That's what I think too. I mean, it seems obvious that the only way we're going to save José is if we actually follow him and that boy into the forest, right?"

"Emily," Maggie whispers. "I think it's really great that you want to save José, but the forest is dangerous. There's something awful going on in there; I can feel it. And José ... well, he's probably already dead."

"I don't think so." Emily's voice rises with excitement. "Did you see the way the trees opened up for him? It's like they knew what he wanted. And how when we're cutting them, if we fight it's way harder, but if we just stand there we don't get nearly as tired. And you, Maggie." She looks over at her triumphantly. "You never cut the vines, and they avoid you completely."

"Because Danny slices them before they get near her," Trevor mutters.

Emily ignores him. She steps closer and lowers her voice. "It's like they have minds, like they understand us. They seem to know what we want, and if all we wanted was José and not that stupid water I'll bet they'd let us in there after him."

"Sure they'd let us in." Trevor crosses his arms and steps backwards. "Just like they let José in. Twenty feet and then kapow! We'd be dead. They have minds all right, Emily. Evil minds."

"I think you're wrong. I think they would let us in. What do you think, Danny?"

"Er ..." My eyes are adjusting to the darkness and I

can see Emily clearly now, her fingers fidgeting with a piece of white cloth, her hopeful eyes pleading with me. I have to look away. "I think Trevor's right. José's gone, Emily. Sorry."

———∞———

THE NEXT MORNING Emily pushes her way to the front of the mess hall line and sits at a table with a bunch of kids from the No-Wits. She won't look at us. She won't talk to us.

"Hey, Emily," Maggie calls when we're piling into the mail trucks on the way to the forest, but Emily stares straight ahead and walks past us to a truck farther up the line.

Maggie gazes after her. "She's mad at us."

"Let her be," Trevor replies. "There is no way I am risking my neck just to go after some stuck-up idiot who was too stupid to stay out of trouble."

Emily won't talk to us at the forest either. She grabs a machete and then takes up a position with another group. From where we're standing, I can hear her whispering to a couple of them.

"Are you crazy?" One of the girls steps away and shakes her head sharply from side to side. "No way!" The rest of the group turn their backs on Emily. She moves along and starts whispering to someone else.

She won't stand with us in the soup lineup, or eat with us afterwards. She doesn't ride with us in the truck back to the compound. At supper, she comes to the mess hall late and stands at the back of the line. Her cheeks are puffy and red.

She fills her plate and stands staring at the rows of tables. Maggie points at an empty chair, but Emily ignores her. Instead she peers from one group of Lily Brookers to the next. Finally she tosses her plate down, slumps into the chair beside Maggie, and drops her head onto the table.

"I've asked every single person here and nobody is willing to go with me to find José. Not a single, measly person. Not one."

"Why don't you go alone?" Trevor suggests, his mouth stuffed full of stewed tomatoes (which would taste better, he said after his first bite, with a dash of Antarctic sea salt and some fresh basil, torn, not cut).

"Because." The anger falls from Emily's face and her chin begins to quiver. "I'm afraid to go alone." With that, her shoulders heave and tears begin to pool on the table under her cheeks.

Maggie whispers something.

"What did you say?" Emily wipes her face and blows her nose on her sleeve.

"I said ..." Maggie tears at the skin around her fingernails. "I said, if you want, if you really think it's a good idea, if we absolutely have to ... I'll go with you." She turns quite pale as she says it, but Emily beams.

She jumps out of her chair and grabs Maggie under her armpits, then lifts her and whirls her around until one of the guards shouts a warning from across the room.

"Thank you, Maggie," she whispers, once she's put her

down again. And then she looks somberly from me to Trevor and then back to me again. "At least I have one true friend."

———∞∞———

EMILY CAN'T WAIT to go into the forest after José. The sooner the better, she says. They have to act quickly. If anyone could make it through the forest unscathed, it's Emily, but Maggie I'm not so sure about. Every time I close my eyes I have visions of her crouched on the forest floor, vines twisting around her neck, and her still refusing to cut them away. I don't want her to go, and so I try to come up with reasons why each day isn't the right one for them to leave.

The first morning I focus on the weather; though it's only the end of October, Poplovastan is freezing, and I make sure to remind Emily of that. "It's awfully cold out today. Especially cold. Tonight we should all try to get into the shed to find you two another layer of clothes, and then you can go tomorrow."

The next day it's the food: "Are you sure you feel okay, Emily? I feel terrible. And neither you or Maggie look all that well, either. Something in that supper soup must have gone bad. You don't want to be trudging through the forest with a case of food poisoning."

The third afternoon, after I have concocted a rumor about mail delivery being expected for that evening, the four of us are standing on the farthest edge of the line at the forest when Emily drops her machete and points into the trees.

"Holy hippopotamus! There's a person in there!"

"Sure." I continue chopping at a striking vine, but then I see it too—a flash of movement a few feet away from us, a human face. I drop my knife and take a step back. Trevor and Maggie turn to see what we're staring at, and then drop their knives too.

José? That's my first hope, but it definitely isn't him. It's a man with curly brown hair, small brown eyes, unruly eyebrows, and skin the smooth brown color of clay. He's wearing a worn striped shirt, faded blue trousers, and boots that reach almost to his knees. Beside him, clutching his hand, is a small girl. A brown fur-collared coat hangs down to her ankles. The sleeves are rolled up so that her fingers poke out underneath. When the two of them are almost close enough that I could reach out and touch them, the girl looks up and smiles at the four of us. The trees sway away from them both, or gently brush at their sides as they pass. The vines lie still at their feet.

"How did you do that?" Emily asks them, when they are beside us. The man says nothing, just pushes through the final row of trees and turns onto the road. At the last moment the girl stretches out her hand and lets her fingertips brush my arm. She smiles again before she turns away. I rub the spot of warmth she pressed into the sleeve of my Lily Brook blazer.

"Do you feel that?" Maggie asks. At first I think she's talking about the girl's touch, but she's staring into the forest. "The trees are so peaceful now."

Trevor looks at her skeptically, but he doesn't argue.

No one else stops working. No one else even sees them.

THAT NIGHT, just as I'm falling asleep, Emily calls from behind the curtain again, insisting Trevor and I wake up and meet with her.

"So," she demands, when we're both facing her through the bars. "Are you finished with your excuses? Will you boys come with us now?"

"What if we do?" Trevor asks. "And we get stabbed to death by tree branches, or strangled by vines, or eaten by wild animals? What if we die of exposure, or starvation? What if we do find José, but his body has been torn into a million pieces all over the forest floor?"

"What about you, Danny? You want to join our expedition?"

"Your what?"

"Expedition," Emily says. "You know …"

But I'm not listening. In my head, I'm remembering the time I told Father about my dream of being an explorer. "And I'll go on expeditions all over the world," I had told him. "And I'll never be scared." I wouldn't have been much more than six or seven at the time, yet now that I'm older and I do have a chance to explore someplace new, I'm terrified. What if I get killed in there?

As if reading my mind, Maggie says, "The man and his daughter didn't even get hurt by the trees."

"And besides," Emily adds, "isn't it worth it to try?"

I think about the little girl in the forest again, and of the way the trees shifted aside for her and her father. And then I think about what Emily said. She's right, probably. Maybe if we go into the forest we'll find a way out of Lily Brook; we never will if we stay. And if we do stay here, will it really be better than dying in the woods? What if I live until I'm eighty, in Lily Brook, and spend every day until then fighting the forest, and eating supper soup for lunch, and sleeping on a sawdust pillow? What if I never see my home and my family again?

"I'll go," I say to Emily, and she lets out a hoot and grabs my arm through the bars.

"I can't stay here by myself," Trevor whines. "There's nobody else worth talking to."

"So come with us."

Trevor sticks his thumb into his mouth and starts to bite at his nail. "Fine," he says at last. "I will."

XVIII

EMILY SAYS WE SHOULDN'T BRING WEAPONS: not knives, not axes, definitely not machetes.

"If the forest thinks we want to hurt it, it will hurt us."

Maggie, of course, has no problem with Emily's rule, and I'm willing to go along with it too, but Trevor's more resistant.

"You didn't mention this was a suicide mission, Emily," he mutters.

When she ignores him he crosses his arms over his chest. "I'm not going, then. No knife, no way."

Emily turns to me, and I shrug my shoulders. "Fine," she relents. "A small one. *If* you hide it."

And so the next morning when we arrive at the forest,

we're the only ones who don't rush to the frost-covered tool pile. Only Trevor does. He bends down and grabs a tiny knife while the rest of us wait for him at the edge of the forest.

"Here." Emily yanks the knife away once he joins us. She wraps the blade in a small piece of cloth she pulls from her pocket, then hands it back.

"What's this cloth?" Trevor unwraps the fabric and lifts José's torn Lily Brook shirt collar up for Maggie and me to see. "Aha!" he shouts, when he recognizes it. "You've recruited us because you have the hots for the ballerina."

"Danseur," Emily mutters, staring at her feet. Her cheeks flame pink.

"Shhh." Maggie shakes her head at Trevor. "We will save him. I know we will, Emily."

———✺———

WE ARE ALL HUDDLED at the edge of the forest, discussing the best point of entry, when Bob strides over.

"Where are your tools?" he demands.

"We're going in." Emily glares at him, daring him to challenge her.

"You're what?" A smile spreads across Bob's face.

"I said the four of us are going into the forest, so if you don't mind, we'd really rather you left us alone."

"Hey, Bernice." Mother Ma'am turns around. "Hey, guys," Bob calls to the rest of the guards. "Get a load of this. These little twerps are going into the forest."

There's a commotion as the guards jump from the mail

trucks and rush towards us, wanting a front-row view of the action, but except for a few gasps the rest of the Lily Brookers are quiet. They all fix their gazes at the forest and hold their tools ready. Or, rather, all of them but Uncle Ernst, who clasps my arm with one hand and Emily's with the other and leans down so his mouth is level with our ears.

"Let's think rationally for a moment, kids. Sure, working in the forest is frustrating, and losing a friend makes everything all the more difficult, but—"

"We're going." Emily pulls her arm away. "We're not afraid."

"But, Emily!" Ernst cries as he lets go of me and attempts, unsuccessfully, to block Emily's way. Emily marches to the very edge of the forest, then looks over her shoulder and motions for the rest of us to follow.

"Danny," Ernst seizes my arm again, "don't you remember what I told you about residents who go into the forest?" I nod, but he continues anyway. "They never come back!"

"But don't you wonder if maybe they could have, but just didn't want to?" And then, even though I realize as soon as the words leave my mouth that they might hurt him, I add, "Isn't it better to be brave than to be scared for the rest of your life?"

Ernst doesn't respond, but lets go of my arm. Emily takes a step closer to the forest, and then another. We all trail behind her. Just as before, the trees part when she steps past the forest's edge.

When we're about fifteen paces in, Uncle Ernst calls out to us weakly. "Can't we talk this through?"

"No." Emily whirls to face him. "*We* don't intend to waste twenty years at Lily Brook." She keeps walking and so do we. Then the shaking starts, and the rustling starts. I close my eyes and Maggie grabs for my hand, and just before it all goes dark I hear someone running towards us. "You can't go alone! You're only children. You'll need help."

※※

I AM THE FIRST to open my eyes. The rest of them are huddled in a tight circle on the forest floor with their hands over their heads: Maggie, Emily, Trevor, and Uncle Ernst—who must have reached us just before the shaking started. They're all breathing hard, but they're still very much alive. And so am I, for that matter. I hold my arms out in front of me and roll up my sleeves—not even a scratch.

"Hey, you guys."

Emily's eyes flutter open. She stretches out her arms and legs and then glances around her. From the inside, the forest is still dark, but not quite as dark as it seems from the edge. I can make out the shapes of the closest trees surrounding us. They all look as if they are bent towards us, listening or watching.

"Uncle Ernst?" Emily walks over to him and touches his shoulder, but he keeps his head pressed between his knees. Maggie and Trevor unfold themselves, though. As

Trevor gazes at the trees towering over us, Maggie slides over so she is pressed against Uncle Ernst. She takes his hand. "We're all safe," she whispers.

When Uncle Ernst finally opens his eyes, the first words out of his mouth are a question: "Which way do you suppose is out?"

"It doesn't matter. We're not leaving." Emily crosses her arms over her chest. She looks as menacing as Mother Ma'am.

"You kids didn't seem the type to believe in wishing wells. If I had known you were planning something like this, I would have kept better watch. It's been years since we lost an Ugly." He shakes his head sadly. "Besides José," he adds, when Emily glares at him.

"We didn't come for the well."

"Then what?" Ernst looks confused.

"We came to find José."

"Oh, Emily." Ernst reaches for Emily's hand but she pulls it away. "You dear, sweet girl. You saw it: the shaking, the quivering, the trees thumping him over the head. All of them leaning in towards him and then …" He pauses. "Silence."

"If you're saying he's dead, you're wrong," Emily replies. "We survived, didn't we?"

"That is a curious truth, indeed." Uncle Ernst steps towards the nearest tree and runs his palm down its trunk. He bends down and scoops a pile of dirt from the forest floor, sifting it through his fingers and examining the rocks and twigs, and the small clear beetle he has unearthed. "And, I must admit, I have always wondered what one would find here if one managed to make it into the forest alive."

I step closer to Ernst and watch the beetle scuttle across his palm. Its shell is perfectly transparent—it looks like it could be a picture from one of Brittany's science books: inner workings of bug.

"Never mind that." Emily pulls me away from Uncle Ernst. "We have to start looking. We need to cover as much ground as we can before night comes." She closes her eyes and spins around on one foot with her arm pointing out in front of her. When she comes to a stop and opens her eyes, her arm is jabbed out to the left of where we're standing. "This way first." But as she says it, the trees to the left of us seem to puff out their branches and knit them together, barring our way through.

"Oh my goodness, they're trapping us," moans Trevor. All the branches have twisted together to form a thick wall. There's no way to get under them, there's no way to get over them, there's no way to get around them, and there's certainly no way to get through them.

"Hey, look." Maggie is facing the other direction. I follow the line her arm points into the forest. A thin path has cleared in front of her for as far as my eyes can see. Even the vines that are usually twisted across the ground seem to have shriveled up.

"To the right then." And Emily begins to march.

The rest of us follow, Uncle Ernst and Maggie bringing up the rear, through the clumps of spiny-barked trees and strangling vines, and the patches of spiky moss that dot the forest floor. None of them push against us to cut slices into our skin, and none of them swing hard to throw us to the ground. But the forest does change. It doesn't become darker the deeper we get, as I had expected. Nor does it become colder. There's frost on the ground, and icicles on the bottom of some of the branches, but we are warm enough in our Lily Brook blazers. What does happen is that the farther we walk into Poplova Forest, the more alive the forest seems to become.

It's no longer only the trees that appear to be watching us; there are rustles and whispers behind the trees and among their branches. Small brown eyes that stare at us from within the forest's depths blink shut the second we twist around to see who, or what, they belong to. Flashes of movement skid to a halt when we whirl around to investigate. A few times I think I see a head of curls duck behind a tree, and at one point I swear that someone in a fur-collared coat is following me, but these visions always disappear when I stop to take a better look. And although I don't admit it to anyone, twice I think I see my mother watching from behind a clump of hanging vines—the first time, though, it's just a slender tree trunk and the second, the shadow of a moss-covered rock.

"Who's there?" Trevor calls out now and then, but every time he does, the sounds stop and the forest grows unnaturally still again.

The branches continue to part for us, making a path that leads us deeper still into Poplova Forest. At first the mountain is just a rocky mound in the distance, but it grows and grows until the base takes up the entire sky in front of us. When we crane our necks to look for the top, we see nothing but rocks and cliffs and still more rocks and cliffs.

"Do you think this path leads towards the cave after all?" Trevor whispers. No sooner do the words leave his mouth than we step out of the trees and into a clearing. The base of the mountain is before us, and cut into it is a small opening. Guarding it is a man in a ragged skirt made of woven bark and black fabric—black fabric with a gold monogrammed "LB" in the center.

XIX

"BRUNO!"

The man is tall and very thin. His knotted gray hair is
full of sticks and leaves and hangs well past his shoulders.
When he hears his name, he whirls around to face us, then
draws a machete up and slices the air with its blade.

"Don't move another inch." His face is sallow, and
there are dark circles around his eyes.

One glimpse of the machete blade is enough to make
Trevor and Maggie duck behind the nearest rock. I'm
not all that keen on walking closer to the cave either, but
Uncle Ernst continues towards the man. "Bruno, don't
you recognize me?"

"Sure I do." Bruno is still twirling the machete around.

"You're one of them thieves. You want some of my water, but you're not getting any. It's mine."

"It's me, Ernst, from the Uglies."

"Hefflebauer?" The man drops his machete slightly but keeps his position at the center of the cave's entrance. "That really you?"

In answer, Uncle Ernst reaches for the man's free hand and pumps it up and down, then pulls him close and claps his back in a hug. "All this time, I thought you were dead."

"Nah," the man says, beaming. But then he frowns and takes a step backwards. "But you don't expect, since we were friends and all, that I'm going to offer up the well water, do you?"

"Hey ..." Uncle Ernst holds up his arms. "Bruno, we're not here for the water, really. We're here because these kids are looking for their friend. Dark hair, glasses, chubby face. Have you seen any kids around here lately?"

"Oh, I've seen kids all right. The forest is crawling with them. And all of them are looking to steal water from my well. But I got here first and the well is mine." He leans back, then coughs a deep rasping cough. He sputters and chokes until he is bent nearly in two.

Crawling with them. At these words Emily turns to face me—a look of triumph on her face. But I hardly have time to think about what Bruno might mean before he makes a strange strangled sound and then horks a large glob of spit onto the ground by his feet, the effort of which makes him shake and gasp for breath.

"Are you okay?" Maggie rushes towards him, but Bruno lifts the machete again and holds it over his head. It slips from his fingers and clatters against the rocks. He watches it fall and then lets himself slide down the rocks until he's sitting in a pathetic heap on the dusty ground.

"Do you swear," he whispers, looking up at Uncle Ernst, "that you're not here for the well?"

"On my own grave."

"And them?" Bruno points at the four of us. Maggie is crouching beside Bruno, rubbing his back, although he seems hardly to notice. Trevor is still half-hidden, his mouth hanging open from the sight of the wild-looking man. Emily is pacing back and forth at the edge of the trees, her eyes on the ground, likely looking for evidence of José. And I'm standing still, trying to pretend I don't feel the tree branch that has come to rest on my back and which is pushing me, gently but firmly, towards the cave.

"Them neither."

"Well, then come, come, help me onto my feet. Last time I fell it took three days and about eighteen handfuls of those translucent spiders before I got my strength back to stand again."

We all step forward to help Uncle Ernst lift Bruno. He makes no effort to stand when we get him onto his feet, but leans against us as if he were asleep or in a faint. It hardly matters though; he is as light as a sack of air. We can feel his joints under his skin.

"Where shall we put you?" Ernst asks.

"Oh, just lean me up against the mouth of the cave. That's where I stand."

"All day?" Trevor gapes at him.

"All day, all night."

"You mean you never move? You always stand there?" At first, I'm certain he can't be serious, but then I notice the moss around the cave entrance. It grows thick everywhere, except for a small human-shaped patch where the rock is clean and smooth.

"At first I didn't stand there, but the forest is crawling with bandits now. I have to stay alert—protect the fortress, guard the castle, bar the intruders."

"Can't we put you inside?" Emily takes a step towards the cave entrance.

Bruno eyes her suspiciously. "Are you certain you're not here for a sip of water, little girl?"

"I'm certain." She draws an "X" on her chest with her fingertips. "Cross my heart."

"I don't like to leave the entrance, too dangerous. But how many of us are there?" Bruno murmurs. "Four of you young ones, Ernst, myself. That makes six. Any of you folks have a weapon on you?"

"I have a knife wrapped up in my pocket," Trevor blurts. Emily glares at him and raises her finger to her lips.

"It's just little," Trevor clarifies. "It's not really a weapon at all." He looks out at the trees, which seem to be bending towards us. "I'm not here to hurt anything. It's a spreading knife. For jams and such." The trees rustle up straight again.

"Fine, then." Bruno nods at Trevor. "Six of us, the machete, and a spreading knife. We should be able to take care of any intruders if they slip inside."

⟶⟶⟶

JUST PAST THE MOUTH OF THE CAVE is a tunnel that leads to a large room. Torches hang at intervals so that everything is bathed in light. The rock walls glisten. On them, carved deep into the surface, are pictures: trees with branches stabbing people through the chest, vines wrapped around people's stomachs and necks, men and women charging towards one another with their fists held in front of them like weapons, and a tangle of people falling into a deep pit. In the center, under the largest torch, a picture of a person with a blank face is carved into the wall. The figure has a cup raised to his lips. Flames seem to leap from his head.

"Did you carve these yourself?" I can't imagine how long it would have taken to make the pictures. The lines are cut much deeper into the rock than in the photographs of petroglyphs I've seen in some of Brittany's books at home.

"Those? Nah, they were here when I first arrived."

"And the torches? Do you keep them lit always?" Emily is standing under one, her face glowing in the light of the flame.

"I don't touch the torches, but they never burn out. Strangest things, they are."

"I remember this." Uncle Ernst is gazing at the far wall.

"Wasn't there a sketch of it in that article your brother gave you, Bruno?" He points to the flaming figure raising the cup.

Bruno shrugs. "Something like it, but I hardly remember. Those papers became bug food years ago."

"Where's the well?" Trevor has wandered over to the far side of the cave.

Bruno points to what first appeared to be a shadow, but is actually a giant hole in the center of the floor. We all stand around it and peer in. I can see nothing but darkness, but from someplace far below, if I tilt my head, close my eyes, and listen very hard, I can hear the silky rustling of water.

"It must be very deep." Emily bends over and picks up a pebble from the floor near her feet, then throws it in. It's nearly ten seconds before we hear a faint splash.

"How did you ever get the water out of there?" I ask.

"I haven't yet."

"But it's been almost twenty years!" Uncle Ernst steps away from the carvings and turns in shock towards Bruno. "You left Lily Brook that very first winter. How long did it take you to find the cave?"

"Oh, two days, maybe three. But I had only just found my way inside when I heard a noise from the entrance. It was a boy from the No-Wits: Horace or Harris, I can't remember now. Must've gone into the forest soon after me. I rushed out there with my machete and guarded the entrance. And I kept guarding it, too, because he was always sneaking up to see if I was still there. 'Bruno, I just want to talk to you,' he would say, but I knew what he really wanted, and I had gotten here first, fair and square. There've been many through the years, crooks that is. I've had to protect the well from all of them."

"So you haven't had even one sip?" asks Trevor.

"Child, if I'd had a sip of that water, do you really think I'd be standing here right now in a bark skirt, with nothing in my stomach but the handful of ants I found under a rock this morning?"

"So why don't you have a drink?" Emily demands.

"Why, to get the water from the well I'd need some way to lower my tin can down."

"But the forest is right out there." I point out the mouth of the cave. "You could make a rope from vines, or strips of bark."

"Every vine rope I've ever made has fallen apart the instant I dragged it in here," Bruno replies. "Something about the air quality in the cave, I suspect. The knots don't hold. And I can hardly go searching the forest for another method. The second I do, someone else will rush in and claim the water for themselves."

"But what good is the well if you can't even get the water out of it?" Emily asks.

"Isn't that obvious?" Bruno's eyes gleam. "The well is entirely mine."

XX

AFTER WE HAVE WANDERED AROUND the cave for a few minutes, tracing the carvings with our fingers and staring into the well, Bruno starts getting antsy. He looks from us to the entrance of the cave, and back to us again.

"We should get back out there," he says. "Besides, I have something you all might be interested in." We follow him out the entrance, and he reaches into a fallen log and pulls out a handful of carved wooden figures.

"Chess men!" Uncle Ernst cries, taking a couple in his hand and admiring them. They are incredible: perfect knights, bishops, castles, a tall crowned man perched on a throne.

"All carved by machete." Bruno reaches into the log

and pulls out still more figures. "Which is no easy task, I assure you."

He and Ernst use a stick to scratch a chessboard into the dirt, and they begin to play. At first, Bruno insists on explaining every move he makes, but the rest of us are too distracted to pay much attention; we want to know about José and the other Lily Brookers in the forest. But Bruno says he has no idea who's been around the cave.

"I don't wait for introductions. The lot of them are thieves."

"And where do they stay?" I can't imagine living in this forest. Even the hard bunks at Lily Brook seem preferable to sleeping on a pile of vines that are quite capable of strangling me at any moment. Or building a house out of branches that fight back.

"Don't ask me. As long as they're out there and not around here I don't give a cat's whisker where they are." But Bruno doesn't sound so certain. He cocks his head to listen to the sounds of the forest, then reaches for his machete, propped on a rock beside him.

Once the sun sets, the torches seem to glow brighter. Maggie and Trevor huddle beneath one in the entrance-way of the cave. I hear them whispering a pact to pinch each other if one notices the other drifting off. The combination of the fierce trees beyond the cave's entrance and Bruno's machete make sleep less than appealing—but within minutes I hear Trevor's slow snores and Maggie's deep, whistling breath.

Bruno lets us spend the night inside, though I notice that

once we're lying down he shifts slightly so he can watch both the forest and us at the same time. But he's a good host. When we wake up the next morning he presents us each with a fistful of translucent worms—a breakfast it must have taken him half the night to collect.

"Haul the lot of those hoodlums back to Lily Brook with you," he calls from the cave entrance when we set off again to look for José. "The less, the merrier."

———ᨆᨆᨆ———

THE TREES DON'T PART to form a path as they did yesterday, and we have to resort to bushwhacking—crawling over rocks, ducking under fallen branches, beating our way through clumps of vines. At first, Emily takes the lead, but when she's in the front, half the turns we take end at impenetrable walls of trees or rocks, or clumps of particularly sharp-looking plants we don't dare attempt to walk through.

Aside from barring our way through it, today the forest leaves everyone alone. Everyone, that is, except me. Just like yesterday, when the branch seemed to want to shove me into the clearing by the cave, I constantly have twigs digging into my back, pushing me in one direction or the other. At one point, a vine wraps around my arm and yanks me sideways. It drops me before I have a chance to scream out to the others, and when it does I notice that I had been heading directly for a deep pit in the forest floor. Surely if I had kept walking I would have landed inside it. Emily and the rest stumble over branches just as often as I do, but in their cases the branches remain still. They don't reach up and give their pant legs a tug mid-trip.

As strange as my special treatment seems, I don't mention it aloud. Instead, I offer to take the lead from Emily. When I'm in the front of the group it's easy to imagine that I'm trampling through parts of the forest that no one has even laid eyes on before. *See, I am an explorer,* I want to tell Father.

Emily is thrilled with my luck in the forest and happy to trail along behind me. She's thrilled about most things, in fact. Bruno's rant about the other Lily Brookers in the forest did wonders for her. Now entirely confident that José is only moments from being rescued, she's back to her usual self: pointing out interesting shadows, speculating about the mysterious forest kingdom that she seems certain is around every corner, exclaiming how beautiful the transparent bugs are and how kindly the forest is treating us.

Maggie and Trevor are less enthusiastic. Maggie says she can feel the forest's unhappiness, and in her attempts to be gentle with it by avoiding trampling on roots and vines, she often stumbles off the trail. She's ripped a hole in the knee of her pants, and has to hobble with one hand in Uncle Ernst's in order to keep up with us. Trevor, who could barely gag down his wormy breakfast this morning, is experiencing such loud stomach rumbles that initially I mistook them for the same rumbling that started when we first entered the forest and I threw myself to the ground with my arms over my head.

After a couple of hours, when the rest of us are able to convince Emily to take a rest, Uncle Ernst lies on the ground digging in the dirt for lunch. He gives Maggie, Emily, and me four worms each, but collects more than a handful for Trevor, which he keeps in his pocket and doles out one by one during the rest of the afternoon. Still, by the time the light turns dusky through the trees, even the see-through slugs on the trail are moving at a faster clip than Trevor is. "We should have just taken some of that water—made a rope of our clothes or something. Then we could have wished for José and he would have appeared."

"And had a machete stabbed clear through us?" With my hand I mimic a blade slicing through Trevor's stomach. "No, thank you."

"It's incredible the life some people are willing to lead in the name of myths and fairy tales," Uncle Ernst sighs.

"You still don't believe it's true?" Emily turns to Uncle Ernst. "After you saw the cave with your own eyes, and the well, and the pictures on the wall, and the torches that are always lit? It has to be true."

"Maybe, Emily. But if it were true it would be a miracle, hardly something to count on. And hardly something to spend one's life searching for or guarding."

"I think it's definitely true," Emily says. "Right, Danny?"

I shrug. I didn't used to believe in magic, but now I'm less certain. Because if a forest picks a fight with a person, and torches burn for years, couldn't it be possible that some wells grant wishes?

"It doesn't matter anyway," Emily says. "Because we need to keep our eyes on the goal, right?"

"Our distressed danseur, José," Trevor mutters.

Emily doesn't answer; she just crosses her arms over her chest and begins to walk faster, so I almost need to jog in order to keep the lead. We walk the rest of the way in silence. The trees begin to make a path for us that loops around the base of Poplova Mountain and then zigzags outwards in wide arcs. The air is so cold it feels like we're snapping through it as we move. My pants have frozen to my skin and my feet are as heavy as tree stumps.

Just before the sun sets completely we enter a clearing with a bright glow in the center. I can hear the hiss and crackle of flames, but also something else. The sound of human voices. We tiptoe forwards, staying deep inside the shadows until we've approached what turns out to be a great bonfire. Around the fire is a crowd of bodies: tall bodies, short bodies, men's bodies, women's bodies, and all of them dressed in worn and ragged Lily Brook uniforms. They perch on stones, lean against stumps, or sit cross-legged on the forest floor. And once my eyes adjust to the dim light I see more people behind them in the doorways of lean-tos built from fallen branches, and dangling between trees in hammocks made of woven vines.

Uncle Ernst steps out of the shadows, and all of the noise around the fire stops.

"Ernst, you old bat," a man with a mud-streaked face calls. "You decided to take a stab at the well at last?"

Uncle Ernst doesn't answer. He's looking from one

ex-Lily Brooker to the next. His jaw hangs slack, and he shakes his head slowly.

"Is this," he finally manages, stepping closer to the bonfire, "is this all of you? I mean, everyone who ever left?"

"Sure." The mud-man nods, sweeping his arm around the circle. "Every last one—except, of course, for old Bruno, standing out there in front of the cave day and night for the last nineteen years."

"And you've been trapped here all along? You weren't able to get back to Lily Brook?"

"Get back to Lily Brook?" Mud-man echoes. "Why on earth would we want to do a thing like that? If you haven't noticed, Ernst, we're only a short walk from the cave. The well is at our fingertips."

I peer around the circle at the clusters of men and women, who stare back with interest. Finally I see a face I recognize near the shadows' edge. His glasses hang crooked and are missing a lens, his cheeks are bruised and cut, and a large bump has sprung from his forehead, but it is definitely José. Emily sees him too.

"José." She runs towards him and seizes his arm in both hands. "We're here to rescue you."

"You're here to what?" He steps back, his lips pursed like he just finished off a can of the guards' latest creation—tuna and horseradish supper soup.

"To rescue you, to bring you back to Lily Brook with us." Emily grins triumphantly, but José peels her fingers from his arm.

"I came here to drink from the well, and I'm not leaving until I do."

"But, José ..." Emily begins.

"And if I did want to go back to Lily Brook, and be the Brooks' slave, and eat slop, and sleep in a room that smelled like armpits and bad breath, I could find my own way there. I certainly wouldn't need to be saved by you, Emily."

"That cross-eyed idiot," Trevor mutters from beside me. And then he's pushing through the crowd until his face is almost touching José's. "Listen. Emily made us all walk into this forest and follow the tree path to the mountain. We found the cave, we found the well, and now we've found you and we're taking you back."

"You what?" The Twit boy who José followed into the forest has been tending the fire with a stick. He swings around now, the branch in his hand stabbing towards Trevor. "Do you mean to say you actually went inside the cave? You actually saw the well?"

"Sure." Emily shrugs. "We saw it."

There's silence as all the ex-Lily Brookers turn to face us, their eyes as round as dinner plates, their mouths hanging open like the slack wooden jaws of Christmas nutcrackers. And then they all begin to speak at once.

"What was it like?" a man who resembles a stick-thin leprechaun calls from the back of the group.

"Oh, please tell us," begs the hunched-over woman beside him.

"None of you have *ever* seen it?" Uncle Ernst looks

like he doesn't know whether to believe them or not. And it does seem impossible. The mountain looms in the distance. It only took us a few hours to make it here from there. And the trees didn't seem to mind *us* reaching the cave.

But they all shake their heads. No one has.

"I got close once," admits a woman with a head of tangled white curls. "But Bruno nearly chopped my ear off with his machete."

"I had one foot inside," says a short, bald man with a beard that skims the forest floor. "But he swung the blade so close to my neck that I turned and ran for my life."

"He's crazy with that thing." Someone in the back taps at his head and makes a face, and the others nod in agreement.

"But if everyone's here but Bruno, well, that's almost one hundred of you. You can't really believe he could take you all on at once," Uncle Ernst says.

"Who said anything about all at once?" A man kneeling beside the fire looks up at Uncle Ernst. A scar as jagged as a lightning bolt stretches across his face. "I'm not taking any of these fools with me to the cave when I get there. They might turn on me, and drink every last drop of the water themselves."

"Oh, yes." The group of women beside him nod.

"Definitely," a wisp-thin man agrees.

"These people are insane," Trevor whispers to me. "Do you think it could be because of their diet? The worms and all?"

I don't answer. I'm watching one of the younger men, who has stood up from his fallen log to address us. "I for one have stayed up every night for the past one hundred nights just waiting for someone to make a break for the cave. Soon as anybody so much as stirs on the ground, I scream out a warning to the others and we all hold him down."

"I haven't slept either," says a woman to his left. "I have to keep my eyes on *him* to make sure he doesn't get up to something when the rest of us are asleep."

"But it's a well *full* of water," Emily and I say at once.

"Surely there's enough for everyone to have a sip or two," Uncle Ernst adds. But no one seems to be listening any longer. They're all looking around the circle at each other suspiciously, just waiting for someone to make a break for the forest.

XXI

THE NEXT MORNING, when we wake up from our mattresses of fallen leaves we pushed together on the forest floor, Trevor asks Emily if we can just leave José where he is and return to Lily Brook without him.

"He obviously doesn't want to be rescued, Emily. So let him stay, let him rot here. Let *him* sleep on rocks and frozen leaves, let *him* eat translucent bugs; I want to go back, have a big can of delicious supper soup, and fall asleep on my nice hard bunk."

Even though just two days ago I'd never have believed missing Lily Brook would be possible, I agree with Trevor. The forest floor isn't all that uncomfortable, but it's hard to sleep when you can feel vines wriggling beneath you. And supper soup sounds almost gourmet after eating worms. Besides, what if Mother comes to rescue me someday? If I were in the forest she'd never find me.

"I'm sorry, children, but it would be impossible for us to return now," Uncle Ernst says matter-of-factly. "We've been gone two nights already. The consequences would be far too great."

"Consequences?" Trevor turns to Uncle Ernst.

"I'm afraid our return would be met with a lengthy holiday in the dungeon. But chin up." He reaches over and pats Trevor on the back. "Together we can surely make a set of bunks just as comfortable as the ones at Lily Brook. And I've heard that roasting the bugs over the fire improves their flavor."

"It's true, then?" I think about José on our first night, and about the boy with the dog photo in his shoe. "There really is a dungeon? And does the King's ghost really live there?"

Uncle Ernst takes a deep breath. "Well, first of all, Danny, a ghost is dead, so he can't *live* in the dungeon. But the fact is, children ... he haunts the place."

"But that's probably just a rumor." Emily's voice comes out high and squeaky; it's clear even she doesn't believe what she said.

"A rumor I've seen with my own two eyes," Uncle Ernst says. "A moaning ghost, wrapped in chains. Bruno and I were thrown into the dungeon when one of the guards found our chess pieces. The cold, dank, rat-infested cell was bad enough, but then the ghost appeared, and began to beat at the bars between us. Believe me, children, you do not want to spend even a minute down there. The forest is a paradise compared to the dungeon."

What must José have thought when he first saw the ghost? He hadn't even been warned.

Beside me Maggie whispers, "Remember when José came back? He didn't stop shaking for days. Maybe it really would be worse if we left the forest."

"But it can't really be hopeless." As I say the words, I get an idea. "The Brooks wouldn't do anything to us if we told them we found the well, would they?" It seems like a great solution to me. Arriving like heroes—the guards and the Royals begging us for details. "Not if we told them how we got there and what it looked like. They wouldn't hurt us then."

"They wouldn't believe us, Danny Boy," says Uncle Ernst. "Not unless we had proof. And we have no proof to give them. But don't despair. I'm sure after a little while this forest will seem like more of a home than Lily Brook ever could have." He's smiling, but only with his mouth. His eyes look tired, and worried, and sad. Maybe he's imagining what life will be like in the forest: hard, uncomfortable, dirty, and hopeless. At least at Lily Brook there was a chance we could be rescued one day, a chance the Brooks would finally lose interest in the well water and set us all free. If we stay in the forest, we'll be here forever.

"But they will believe us, and they will let us back, because we'll have proof. We're taking them some water!" Emily says. She's not wearing her blazer, and her shirtsleeves have been sliced to just above her elbows. I'm freezing just watching her, but Emily doesn't look cold at all; she looks radiant.

"How, exactly?" Trevor rolls his eyes. "Are you going to climb down the well and scoop a tinful yourself?"

Emily motions for us to follow her. A few feet into the forest she bends down and pulls something from the inside of a rotten stump: vines knotted together into a thick coil of rope.

"Fifty-four arm lengths long," she whispers. "I stayed up all night making it. We loop it to one of our soup cans, then drop it down the hole and pull some water up."

"Didn't you hear Bruno?" Trevor is obviously not as impressed as I am by Emily's night labor. "He's tried vine ropes before. They fall apart. And how do you expect to get around him and his machete anyway? Because if you think I'm going to hold him off with my butter knife …"

"But it's not just vines on their own; it's vines and fabric. I knotted them together with pieces of my blazer and my shirt. And we don't need to get around him. We wrap the thing up in our clothes. We distract him. Someone drops the can down and fills it with water, then throws away the vine and sticks the can in their pocket. It's brilliant."

Trevor looks at her doubtfully.

"Come on. You know it's brilliant."

"It might work," I say. "It's worth a shot."

"And they'd have no reason to keep anyone at Lily Brook anymore." Emily is listing off the advantages to her plan. "The Royals could make their stupid wishes and go wherever it is they want to go, and everyone at Lily Brook would be free."

"Maybe." Uncle Ernst looks skeptical.

"But if we do get some water, shouldn't we just drink it ourselves?" Trevor has taken a step towards the vine and is examining Emily's knots. "Then we could *wish* everyone free."

"Best to avoid that, Trevor," Uncle Ernst says. "The water has been stagnant for years; it could be poisonous. And there's no telling what powers it has."

"I'd just wish myself healthy again. And I'd wish for my own jet to fly home in. A jet with a stocked kitchen. And I'd wish …"

I clutch the button in my pocket. If I had only one wish, I know exactly what it would be.

⸎

ON OUR WAY BACK to the mountain, we walk past the grid of lean-tos and woven-vine tarps that make up the ex-Lily Brooker's camp. We pass a handful of people peeling back the moss from tree trunks and fallen logs to search for bugs, but most of the others are at the bonfire, where they are skewering their six-legged finds on sticks and roasting them in the flames.

"I can't watch this." Trevor sits down on a boulder and buries his head in his lap. "The sooner we get out of here, the better."

"Get out of here?" Mud-man, who is scraping through

the hard dirt beside the boulder with a tree branch, digging for worms, stops and looks up at us. "Where would you go?"

"Back to Lily Brook." As soon as the words are out, the activity around the fire stops. All the ex-Lily Brookers turn in our direction.

"You're really going back there?" Mud-man is incredulous. "When we're so close to the well?"

"We're not the type who counts on myths and fairy tales." Emily glances at Uncle Ernst.

"And Bruno?" The leprechaun man wants to know. "Will you say good-bye to him first?"

"Probably."

"What happened when you saw him yesterday?" José is taking an interest in our visit for the first time. "When he let you see the well, did he leave the front of the cave to go inside with you or did he stand guard the whole time at the entrance?"

"He came in with us," Emily replies.

"That's interesting …" José says.

"You know, if you came back to Lily Brook with us you could meet him along the way and see the cave for yourself." Emily winks at me, obviously proud of her new tactic, but José is no longer paying attention.

"Very interesting," he says again, and he glances behind him and takes a step backwards. And then, out of the corner of my eye, I see someone leave the circle and creep towards the edge of the forest. But no one notices. They're all staring into the forest themselves.

José takes another slow step backwards, and then another. When he reaches the edge of the clearing he turns and starts to run, weaving through the trees.

"José!" Emily shouts after him. "Come back!" But he doesn't even slow down, and neither do the rest of the ex-Lily Brookers, who are all charging towards the trees, leaving the roaring fire unattended.

"Do you think they're heading to the cave?" Trevor asks, once they've all disappeared among the foliage and we're stamping out the flames.

"I suspect they'll hide in the woods and then track us." Emily pulls her vine rope from its hiding place and drags it behind her. "We'd better get going."

❦

ON OUR WAY BACK to the cave, the trees lean away from us, making a wide path in the direction of the mountain.

"Something bad is about to happen." Maggie walks slowly, with her eyes on the branches that hang over the trail.

"Nothing bad will happen at all," Emily assures her. "We're about to set everyone at Lily Brook free!"

"But the trees are so tense and anxious."

"They're not anxious, Maggie; it looks like they're excited. They're making a path for us straight to the mountain. They want us to reach the well." Emily is right; the path the trees are making is direct, and within minutes the cave comes into view.

"I'm still not certain about this," Uncle Ernst says,

as we stand at the edge of the clearing and watch Bruno leaning on his machete in the cave's entrance.

"Well, I'm certain about not wanting to eat another meal of see-through worms." Trevor pulls his tin can from his pocket and fastens it to the end of the rope. Then he takes off his blazer, wraps it around the vines, and hands it back to Emily.

Uncle Ernst lets out a deep breath of air. "Fine," he says. "I'll distract him. But you all better work quickly."

XXII

"BACK SO SOON?" As we step into the clearing at the base of the mountain, Bruno greets us from the same position he was in when we left him.

"We're leaving," Uncle Ernst explains. "Returning to Lily Brook. The kids wanted to go right away, but I thought maybe we could play another game first. There's not a single worthy opponent back at Lily Brook."

"Wasn't that always the truth." Bruno smiles and drops his machete, and Ernst reaches into the hollow log for the carved chess pieces. The rest of us perch beside them on a boulder and ask Bruno questions: Has he ever seen an animal in the forest? Do all the bugs taste the same? Doesn't he miss having baths? After a while, he is so absorbed in the game that he doesn't seem to hear us, and responds only with grunts or waves of his hand. Uncle Ernst glances over and jerks his head towards the entrance of the cave. We don't need to be told twice.

While Maggie and Trevor remain perched on the boulder, Emily and I sneak into the cave. She unwraps the rope and tiptoes towards the well while I stand in the shadows of the entrance, my eyes on the machete blade propped on the rock near Bruno—filtered rays of sunlight reflecting off the rusting edge.

Emily has just started to lower the can into the well when there's a commotion somewhere at the edge of the clearing.

"Get back! I was here first!"

"You get back." I step outside in time to see Mud-man shove a frail-looking woman to the ground. "Or I'll wish for you to disappear, I swear I will."

Trevor and Maggie have jumped up to block Bruno's view of the cave, but Bruno is looking elsewhere. He's fumbling for the handle of his machete. "Violence just isn't the answer," I hear Uncle Ernst murmur "… important to be rational …" But once the weapon is in his hands, Bruno stands and turns towards the scuffle and starts slicing the blade through the air.

I duck back into the cave.

"Put the rope away," I hiss at Emily, and she throws Trevor's blazer over the vines and steps backwards just as Mud-man lunges through the entrance, with Bruno tailing him, his machete gripped in both hands.

"Bruno, stop!" Uncle Ernst bursts through the entrance after them, seizing Mud-man with one hand and Bruno with the other. The machete clatters to the ground, and when Bruno tries to reach for it he tumbles in a heap. He clutches Uncle Ernst's leg and tries to pull himself upright, but he has hardly any strength left. When Ernst steps away, towards the group of ex-Lily Brookers now choking the entrance of the cave, Bruno's fingers slip off his pant leg.

"This water is mine!" Mud-man's face is streaked with even more dirt than before, as is the front of his Lily Brook uniform. It looks as if he made the journey from the clearing entirely on his stomach. "Now, if you'll excuse me …" He wrenches free of Uncle Ernst, then pushes him against the wall of the cave and charges for the well. When he reaches it, he kneels for an instant, staring into its depths.

"Get away," croaks Bruno, who is still lying on the ground, now yanking at my pant leg. I turn to Uncle Ernst, wanting to ask if I should help Bruno up, but Uncle Ernst isn't watching. Instead, he has stationed himself at the entrance of the cave, trying to direct traffic.

"Careful, stop that, slow down now …" But no one's listening. Leprechaun-man manages to slip past. He gallops for the well, slowing only when he reaches the edge. It's possible he even tries to stop, but at that moment the crowd bursts through the entrance and he is pushed from behind. He collides with Mud-man and the two of them seem to hover above the well for a moment—Leprechaun-man's long gray beard streaming behind him—before they both disappear. One by one the rest of the ex-Lily Brookers follow suit. They stop to stare into the mouth of the well, then are shoved in by the surging, struggling crowd.

Uncle Ernst tries to pull some of the group back, but there's no use. He gets trampled himself, and Trevor and I have to push our way through the crowd of shoving bodies to reach him. When we do, he waves us away, motioning instead for us to do something about the group of ex-Lily Brookers plummeting into the well.

But what can we do? We're not strong enough to hold anyone back, and though surely Ernst has an idea or two, it's impossible to hear his directions over the cacophony. Screeches and splashes echo off the walls. I look over to Emily for help, but she and Maggie are busy pinning José to the ground.

Then, almost at once, the screeches fade and a final series of splashes sound. Only José's forest companion, the boy from the Twits, is left staring down in amazement at the black pit in front of him.

"Get away," José yells, struggling to break free.

"Step back," demands Bruno, clawing himself upright against the wall.

But the Twit boy is pulling his can from his pocket. He kneels beside the well and sticks his arm in as far as he can reach.

Then Bruno is upright and charging towards him, and José shoves Emily off and follows suit. They're like a couple of bowling balls aimed to knock over the last standing pin.

"Look out!" But Emily's words come too late. Bruno head-butts the Twit boy in the stomach, and José shoves Bruno from behind. All three of them topple forwards until—splash, splash, splash—they've disappeared.

By the time the five of us reach the edge of the well we can no longer even hear the echoes of their screams.

"Hello!" I holler down the hole.

"Hello-hello-hello," calls my own voice back to me.

I bend down and dig around in my sock until I find the button, pull it out and clutch it tightly in my fist. What would Mother do? Run for help? Climb down the side of the well? No matter what kind of problem I had, she always knew how to solve it. But this problem is way bigger than a sick pet turtle, or a collapsed tree fort. And Mother is thousands of miles away.

"Catch this!" Emily takes the vine rope and throws it over the side. The rope unfurls inside the hole, then hangs there limply. When she finally winds it back up, the can isn't even wet.

"Hey, give me that rock." Before I can say anything, Trevor grabs the button from my hand and hurls it down the well.

"Trevor!" But he shushes me and points his ear towards the hole. There is silence for about ten seconds, followed by a quiet *sploosh* as Mother's button disappears for good.

"They must have sunk right to the bottom." Trevor

bites his lip and shakes his head. "I thought maybe they'd clogged the thing up."

I look down at my shoes and pretend to rub some dirt out of my eyes, so no one will notice the tears. But nobody's paying attention to me anyway. Emily has thrown herself to the ground, and the rest of them are kneeling beside her, stroking her hair and resting their hands on her shoulders.

"I ruined everything," she wails. "Instead of rescuing José, I drowned him—along with all the rest of the ex-Lily Brookers. And my idea with the stupid vines wouldn't have worked anyway, because I made the rope too short. Now we'll never be able to get any water to bring back to the Royals." She pulls the tin can off the vine and throws it to the ground, and it rolls to a stop beside my foot.

I stare at the rusted can a moment, and then stoop to pick it up. When I do, a splash of water drops into the can, filling it halfway to the top.

XXIII

AT FIRST I think the cave's ceiling must be dripping, but the ground below me is dry. Just to check, I stretch my arm out towards the hole, and sure enough another large splash leaps from the well and tops up the can. A splash of the same water that drowned a forestful of ex-Lily Brookers. The same water that swallowed Mother's button. Water no one could pay me to drink—magic or no magic.

"Anyone want some?" I hold the can out to the others, and they stare at me in disbelief.

"How did you do that?" Maggie asks.

I shrug, then offer her the can, but she won't take a sip. Neither will Emily or Uncle Ernst. Even Trevor—who had so many wishes, and who rarely turns down something to eat or drink—shakes his head. We all look towards the hole.

"At least now we can try to get back to Lily Brook," Trevor says, after a long stretch of silence. "Before the rest of us die here."

"Let's go, then." Emily stands up and motions for us to follow her, but she's lacking the enthusiasm she had two days ago when she led us into the forest. She sounds like she might burst into tears at any moment.

This morning I had thought that a can of well water would solve all our problems, but now we have one and things are even worse than before. I can't wait to get out of this forest. I stand up too, and hand Emily the can, and we all leave the cave and walk across the clearing. The trees lean towards us, rustling whispers from one to the next, but as soon as we reach the edge of the glade, they swoop aside, making a wide path for us away from the mountain.

"Thank you." Maggie runs her fingers down the bark of the one closest to her.

We walk in silence, Emily in the lead.

Maggie breaks the quiet after a few minutes. "Your rope didn't fall apart, Emily. That was really great. And maybe all the Lily Brookers got water in their mouths when they fell. Maybe they all got their wishes."

"Maybe." But Emily sounds doubtful. So am I. Trevor was right all along; we never should have come here.

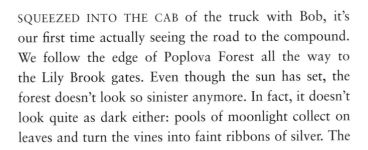

THE SUN HAS ALMOST SET when we reach the edge of the forest, and the last mail truck is pulling away from the side of the road.

"Wait!" Trevor starts to sprint towards it. "Hey, wait up!"

The truck screeches its brakes and Bob jumps from the driver's door. His eyes widen as he looks from Trevor to the rest of us.

"How did you … What did you …?"

Emily holds out Trevor's soup can. "We found the well."

Bob tries to snatch the can from her hand, but she holds it behind her back. "If you touch any of us I swear I'll dump this water on the ground. Now let us in and drive us to the Royals."

Bob opens his mouth but then closes it without saying a word. He nods, goes around to the back, and opens the door. Two rows of Uglies stare out at us.

Emily shakes her head, reaches for the door, and slams it shut. "The front."

SQUEEZED INTO THE CAB of the truck with Bob, it's our first time actually seeing the road to the compound. We follow the edge of Poplova Forest all the way to the Lily Brook gates. Even though the sun has set, the forest doesn't look so sinister anymore. In fact, it doesn't look quite as dark either: pools of moonlight collect on leaves and turn the vines into faint ribbons of silver. The trees aren't waggling their sharp branches at the truck as we pass; they stand upright, perfectly still. At one point I think I see the man in the worn striped shirt and the little girl in the brown fur-collared coat waving to us from the forest's edge, but it's likely just the shadows playing tricks on me.

Bob drives in silence, though every so often he sneaks a look at Emily, pressed against the passenger door with the tin can full of well water in her lap.

He stops the truck at the compound gate and opens his door.

"Where are you going?" Emily demands.

"Thought I should let the rest of those Uglies out before we head to the castle."

Emily narrows her eyes at him and shakes her head. "No need."

He shrugs and slams the door shut, then starts the engine again. We follow the compound wall until we reach the driveway by the castle door.

"You can let them out now."

"I think instead we'd better ..." But before Bob can argue Emily tips the can in her lap ever so slightly so that a drop spills out and hits the floor.

"Okay, okay." Bob jumps from his seat, and we slide out after him and follow him to the back of the truck. When he opens the door, the others file out slowly, nudging and whispering to one another.

"Now you may announce our arrival." The other Uglies look on in shock as Bob turns around and does just what Emily has instructed. He walks towards the door, and the rest of us trail behind him. When he reaches the nameplate he presses his finger on the button beneath it.

"Who's there?" bellows a man's voice.

"It's Bob, sir."

"What do you want?"

"It's the group of Uglies who took off into the forest. They came back, and they claim they've got a can of water for you." The door swings open and Mr. Richard Brook appears on the other side.

"Hand it over." He thrusts his wrinkled hand towards Bob.

"Daddy, you said me first." The Brooks' daughter slithers past her father and grabs at Bob's arm. "Where is it?"

Bob points behind him to Emily, who's holding the can out in front of her, balanced on the flat of her palm. All the Brooks are in the doorway now and they stumble over each other in an attempt to snatch it.

The can wobbles as Emily swings her hand from left to right.

"Careful!" they screech. "Stop that!"

Which she does—suddenly. A sploosh of water tips out and falls onto the grass.

"No!" The Brooks' daughter dives underneath the can and feels around the grass on her hands and knees.

"I'll give this to you," Emily holds the can towards Mr. Brook, "on one condition. You need to release every resident from the Lily Brook compound."

"I will not!" Mr. Brook takes another swipe at the can in Emily's hand.

"Be careful," she taunts, whirling the water towards the lip. "I may drop it."

"What if you're lying?" demands one of the Brooks' sons. "What then?"

Emily shrugs. "If you don't believe me, I can just drink the stuff myself."

"No!" shouts Mrs. Brook as Emily raises the can to her lips. "Bob, go back to the compound and pile everyone in the trucks. Have them driven here and take them through to the ballroom." She glowers at Emily. "We'll release them from here if the water works. If you're simply tricking us, we'll take you all downstairs to the dungeon."

Trevor starts to shake. "Emily …"

But Emily ignores him. She glares at Mrs. Brook. "Of course." She pushes past the Brook family and enters the house. We follow her down the hall and into the ballroom. The three sofas are still arranged in front of the fireplace. Emily perches herself on the edge of one of them. I look back at the Brook family, but when they make no move towards her I sit down too, and Trevor, Maggie, and Uncle Ernst squeeze in beside us.

"Get the King," Mr. Brook commands his wife. She nods and leaves the room.

"But isn't he the ghost?" I whisper to Uncle Ernst.

He nods gravely, and Trevor moans and clutches his belly. Maggie bites her lips and shuts her eyes. But Emily sits tall on the couch and stares at the Brooks.

When Bob returns, he is trailed closely by Mother Ma'am, Captain Ma'am, and the rest of the Lily Brook guards and residents. Usually when all of us Lily Brookers are together we're spread along the edge of the forest; either that or we're in the dining hall, silently shoveling grits or sheep liver or other equally unappetizing things into our mouths. Five hundred silently chewing people doesn't seem like a very imposing group, but five hundred Lily Brook guards and residents who have been called to the Royals' castle without warning—whispering, gawking, and staring—fill up a room pretty quickly.

Still, I can't really concentrate on the other Lily Brookers. I'm staring at the door Mrs. Brook exited through, waiting for her to reappear with the King's ghost.

XXIV

WHEN THE DOOR at the back of the ballroom swings open, Uncle Ernst gasps, as do some of the other residents. An ancient man in a white nightshirt trails behind Mrs. Brook. His face is very pale, and so wrinkled it's hard to see his eyes. His hair and his long white beard are knotted and tangled. He's as skinny as a paper cut-out, and his bony arms are wrapped with thick iron chains.

As soon as I see him, it's obvious the King isn't a ghost after all. He doesn't float on air, but stumbles and trips over the chains dragging behind him. He doesn't screech and moan, but whimpers each time Mrs. Brook tugs hard at the shackles binding his arms. He doesn't give us taunting looks. In fact, his mouth turns up into a smile when he sees us, standing in front of him. He is only a small, old man, who has wasted away to almost nothing after spending years inside the Brooks' dungeon.

Mrs. Brook gives one final tug, and then lets go. When she does, the King collapses on the floor, wheezing.

"Show it to him," Mrs. Brook barks at Emily.

"Say please," Emily scolds the old woman with her finger. "And get him a chair."

Mrs. Brook winces at the thought. "Pl … pl … please," she finally manages, but it seems like just saying the word has made her want to retch. One of her sons drags a chair over from against the wall and places it beside the man, who pulls himself up, gasping, into the seat.

"And get those off him."

The son glowers but removes the shackles from the King's arms. The old man rubs at his wrists.

Emily places the can of well water on his lap.

"Is this what I think it is?" The King's voice creaks like a rusted door hinge; it does sound almost ghostly. He lifts the can to his nose, sniffs at it, then sticks his pinkie in the water and stirs it around. He pulls his finger out and holds it to his face.

"Don't you dare lick that finger!" one of the Brook sons shouts.

The King ignores him. "How did you ever manage to get this, child?"

Emily shrugs. "Some friends and I went into the forest to look for someone, and we found the well."

At the mention of the word "well," the room erupts

in a flurry of conversation. Out of the corner of my eye I notice the Lily Brook guards and residents inching closer, forming a tight circle around us. The King keeps his eyes on Emily. He squints at her for a long moment. "Very interesting."

"Are you certain it's real?" Mr. Brook's beady eyes gleam.

"I've never seen water from the well before, but I've heard about it. It doesn't hold a reflection like regular water. It's always very cold to the touch, no matter how warm the air around it is. It feels almost silky." He dips his finger into the can again. "I would say this water is very real."

"Then hand it over this instant!"

"Just a moment." The King holds up his hand, motioning for the Brooks to step back. "There's something you should know before you take a drink from this can."

"What? Hurry up, old man. Spit it out."

"That well has a history. It was dug many years ago by a woodcutter, the son of one of Poplovastan's most famous wizards. He and his daughter were walking home through the forest when the girl took ill. It was winter and just past nightfall—the moon was behind the clouds and it was cold and dark. The man, tired from carrying his daughter, was afraid he would lose his way. When he saw the entrance to the cave he decided they should spend the night there, and return home in the morning."

The Brooks hover over the King, ready to seize the can as soon as he finishes speaking, but Emily has her hand on the rim and glares at them, daring them to take it.

They don't. Probably because they know as well as I do that she'd tip it if they tried.

"The forest in those days was different. It was lush and green, and the moss that covered the ground was worn thin along the paths the Poplovastanis used to cross from one side of this small country to the other. There were many birds and animals, a number of species that couldn't be found elsewhere, and most were tame and gentle. The bugs were brightly colored—not pale from a life lived in darkness like the ones that exist today."

As soon as the King mentions the pale bugs, I start feeling nauseous, thinking about the worms I had for breakfast yesterday and the handful I ate today when I just couldn't make it any longer without food. I can tell Trevor is thinking the same thing because he wraps his arms around his stomach and starts to groan.

"The girl had a fever and was thirsty," the King continues. "But her father didn't want to leave her alone to search for a spring in the forest. He took off his coat and spread it on the ground, then laid the girl on top of it. He built a fire just outside the mouth of the cave, and from it he lit torches and fixed them to the walls inside, so that the room would be bathed in light and his daughter would not be afraid."

I think of our night in the cave, the group of us huddled beneath the torches attached to the walls. The torches that Bruno claimed were lit even before he arrived. Could the girl's father have lit them all those years before? Is it possible that this story is true? If the King had looked up he would have seen the look of shock that passes between Maggie and me, but he keeps his eyes on the can of water in his lap. He pauses, takes a deep and rasping breath, and continues with his story.

"The girl claimed she could hear water below the rocks. Her father thought she must be hallucinating, but to please her he knelt down and pressed his ear to the ground. Sure enough, he too could hear the sound of water beneath the cave's floor. His daughter begged him to dig a well, a task that seemed impossible. But the man could tell from her glassy eyes and cracked lips that, without a drink, she might not survive the night. He took his knife from his pocket and scraped it against the rock, but the blade did not leave so much as a scratch.

"The girl continued to beg her father for a drink. Her face was flushed and her hair was plastered against her forehead with sweat. The man, who could not bear to see her so unhappy, began to cry. As his tears hit the ground it softened, and the rocks crumbled under his touch. He dug piles of rocks from the floor of the cave, until the hole was deeper than his body, but still he did not reach water."

"Do you really think someone could have dug so far into the rock?" Trevor whispers to me.

I think of the well, so deep that Emily's vine-rope didn't reach the water at the bottom, and shrug. It does seem impossible, but maybe the rock floor of the cave wasn't ordinary rock, just like the trees aren't ordinary trees and the vines aren't ordinary vines. Just like the water might not be ordinary water.

The King pauses and leans back in his chair; the story-telling seems to have exhausted him. The room is silent, as all the guards and Lily Brookers wait for the King to continue, but the Brooks are impatient. All six of them are inching their fingers towards the can.

"I've had enough of this fairy tale," sneers one of the brothers. "I suggest you wrap it up so I can get on with my wishes."

The King takes a deep breath and continues. "The man dug until he could barely see the light above him." He looks around the room as he speaks, ignoring the Brooks, but smiling at the residents who stare attentively up at him. "Finally, he felt the ground beneath him dampen. Moments later a rush of water filled the bottom of the hole. The man took his empty flask from his pocket, filled it, and then climbed up the side of the well to the floor of the cave. By the time he reached his daughter's side he was exhausted; he pressed the flask to her lips and then collapsed beside her on the ground. When the first drop of water touched the girl's tongue, a great warmth rushed through her, and at once strength was returned to her body.

"'Father,' she cried. 'I am well again.' But her father did not reply. He did not make even the faintest sound. The girl pressed her head to her father's chest and listened hard, but there was only silence. He had drained the love from his heart and used it to dig the well and climb back up with the water. There was no life left inside him."

The Lily Brook guards and residents are still leaning towards the King, waiting for him to continue, but the Brooks stop their eye-rolling and begin to laugh aloud.

"You expect us to believe this nonsense?" hoots the Brook daughter. The King pauses, then nods grimly at her. And I *do* believe him. I can tell my friends do too. Maggie started to cry at the King's mention of the father's death, and Uncle Ernst is now holding her hand tightly in both of his. Trevor is staring at the King, transfixed, not even bothering to rub his rumbling stomach. Only Emily seems distracted. She's still clutching the rim of the can and making threatening faces at the Brooks.

"The next morning, a woodcutter heard the girl's cries and discovered her draped over her father's body. He helped her dig a grave for her father at the mouth of the cave and, at her insistence, he kept the torches burning. Then he took her home to his wife and they raised her as if she were their own daughter. She had much happiness with her new family, but she never forgot her father and his sacrifice in Poplova Forest.

"The girl returned to the cave one last time, years later. She leaned over the well and peered into the darkness. 'This water has sprung from my father's tears and lifeblood, and should remain a magical gift for his descendants.' she said aloud. 'But those who wish to use my father's powers for their own selfish aims should beware, for they will be barred from the well by the forest surrounding it. If such a seeker does manage to drink from this well, he will not meet with his deepest desire, but his most terrible fear.' With that, the girl cast the curse, for she had inherited her grandfather's gift for magic and had finally learned how to exercise her powers. The walls of the cave bled tears for the girl and her father, and when they dried they told of the miseries that awaited those who would try to find the well and take the water for themselves."

"The carvings," I whisper to Trevor. If I close my eyes I can picture them exactly: tree branches stabbing at people, strangling vines, men and women charging towards one another with their fists clenched, and a tangle of people falling into a deep pit. "They all came true: the dangerous vines and trees, the ex-Lily Brookers fighting and then falling all at once into the well."

He nods slowly, and then he turns to me and shakes his head. "Not the last one. Not the person with the cup raised to his mouth, and the flames leaping from his head." He looks slightly green as he says it, and I know what he's thinking. I'm thinking it too—maybe that's what will happen next, if the Brooks take a sip from the can.

Even after all the Brooks have done to me, I know I should warn them. I should tell them about the carvings— that I've seen them myself and that the King isn't making things up. But Mr. Brook has already shoved Emily aside and is yanking the can from the King's grasp.

"Why, that's preposterous!" he shouts. "A curse on the water? My greatest fear? You're only saying this so that we'll let you drink it yourself."

"Not at all." The King shakes his head sadly. "I don't share the blood of the wizard-girl, although she was a dear friend of mine for many years. Her granddaughter is the only living relative I am aware of, but she left Poplovastan a long time ago." He eyes Emily again, and then his gaze travels to the rest of us perched on the couch beside her.

"Bottoms up," Mr. Brook bellows, as he tips the can towards his mouth. A fumbling chaos follows, and before I find my voice to shout a warning, the damage has been done. All the Brooks are licking water from their lips.

XXV

AT FIRST, NOTHING HAPPENS. The Brooks close their eyes and cross their fingers, the King frowns and watches them intently, and the rest of us hold our breath and wait for something around us to change—but nothing does. I am almost ready to admit that the forest wasn't special after all, that magic does happen only in fairy tales, when a loud rumble starts beneath us.

Within an instant the floor is shaking, and clouds of dust are being coughed out from the cracks in the golden tiles. Then the tiles themselves begin to dim and crumble, so before I even fully grasp what's happening, there is nothing beneath our feet but piles of dirt and shards of glinting debris.

Then, with a loud roar, the ceiling starts to crumble too, sending showers of dust and plaster to the ground. The air fills with screams, as hundreds of Lily Brookers scatter in every direction. They dive to the floor, or throw themselves against the walls, crouching with their hands over their heads. Some of the guards grab hold of the nearest residents to use as shields. But although chandeliers rattle free and plummet to the ground with huge clumps of ceiling crashing after them, nothing hits anyone. It is spectacular.

Even Emily, crouched on the floor by the King's chair, has screwed her eyes shut. But although I take my blazer off and hold it over my and Maggie's heads, I can't help watching as the ceiling disappears altogether, followed by the walls, until all that is left of the Brooks' luxurious castle are a couple of weathered boards sticking out of the dirt and some pieces of metal littering the ground at my feet. We are sitting under the vast night sky, only a scattering of stars and the full orange moon above us.

"What's happening?" cries Mrs. Brook. "My wish was to be famous the world over, and the richest woman alive. But what is this?"

"Probably your greatest fear." A small smile has crept onto the King's face.

Just then the sofas vanish, and we're all sent sprawling onto the ground. Within moments the rest of the Brooks' furniture disappears or is transformed: the rugs evaporate, a leather ottoman turns into a large boulder, a chandelier that fell onto the dirt becomes a mound of melted candlesticks, and the roaring fireplace changes into a bonfire pit.

The giant trunks that had lined the walls of the ballroom remain intact for a moment, but then the locks shoot off and vanish in a puff of smoke. Some of the trunks fly into the air, tip upside down, and spill their contents before they too evaporate into the night. The suitcases they contained now zip around in the air, skimming the debris on the ground, knocking into rocks and boulders. Their metal locks and buckles shine in the bonfire light. It is beautiful to watch, as if a flock of birds has been released, but it is also terrifying, and I keep my hands over my head.

The cases eventually thump onto the dirt next to their owners, falling open and revealing a jumble of sports equipment and books, stuffed animals and musical instruments. The next clump of trunks to empty and disappear contains clothes: heaps of sweaters, skirts, sandals, and blue jeans. The pair of dress pants Mother picked for me to wear on the journey to Poplovastan just over two months ago lands in my lap, and my shirt and jacket fall on top of them. Yo-yos and photographs and bottle-cap collections and the whole assortment of things Lily Brookers arrived with in their pockets sail through the air and then shower down on us, landing directly in the hands of their rightful owners.

But some possessions have no laps to fall into. Shirts

lie twisted on rocks, and pants are snagged on the shards of metal that litter the ground. A leather bomber jacket lands on the dirt beside me. I try to tuck it underneath my legs before Emily notices, but she turns, frowns for an instant trying to place where she has last seen it, then chokes down a sob as she gathers the jacket into her arms. She whispers apologies into its silk lining. Trevor and I look away, but Maggie slips her hand over Emily's and squeezes tight.

There's not much time to be unhappy though. There is still a pile of trunks left standing and they shake and rattle and thump against the dirt. The lid of one flies open and a small brown parcel hurtles towards us and lands in a small girl's lap. Another box shoots towards us, and another, and another, until the air is a blur of white envelopes and shiny postcards and brown paper packages tied up with string. A small pink envelope lands in my lap, and then a second, and a third—soon my legs are buried in a pile of letters addressed to Mr. Danny Chandelier, in Mother's loopy handwriting. When I lift one to my face I can smell her hand cream.

Three large boxes land on Emily's lap, and she rips them open. Inside are tins of cookies—long since stale—and letters written on stacks of recipe cards held together with elastic bands. In the final package is a bright pink spatula. Emily clutches the handle in both hands and raises the rubber blade to her lips.

Piles of crumpled paper cover the ground as all around me people tear open packages—but not everyone has a lap full of letters. Maggie and Trevor both sit with their hands out, grasping at the fluttering envelopes as they fall towards us, but none come to either of them. Uncle Ernst doesn't even bother looking up. The three of them watch me so closely, as I slide my finger under the flap of one of my letters, that I feel too guilty to open it, and tuck them all into my blazer and out of sight.

"Look, Uncle Ernst—it's a Max Hefflebauer!" Emily waves the pink spatula at him and he takes it and cradles it in the crook of his arm. He closes his eyes and rocks it back and forth.

I turn back to look at the Brooks, and notice one of the sons curled into a ball on the ground with his hands covering his eyes. As I watch him, his pressed beige pants and his crisp collared shirt turn to rags, his hair grows long and knotted, and his skin becomes wrinkled and leathery and stained with dirt.

"How horrible! How awful! How repulsive!" screams another Brook son. He is staring at his hands: the skin on his palms is cracked and callused, and his nails are chipped and yellowed. He opens his mouth to scream again, and I notice his teeth, brown and rotting in his gums.

The Brooks huddle together in a circle, clutching one another and wailing. All but the daughter. She stands apart from her family, trembling, and every so often she looks over her shoulder.

It's as if she is waiting for something.

And she is.

THE BROOK DAUGHTER'S GREATEST FEAR arrives moments later on horseback, with her long hair streaming behind her. She is dressed in blue jeans and a thick winter jacket, and a red woolen hat is pulled down over her ears. She might be older than my mother, but her rosy cheeks and wide smile make her seem quite young. I know instantly where I've seen her before: the back page of the Lily Brook brochure. It's Lily Brook herself.

Lily leaps from the horse and runs towards the Brooks.

"My family!" she cries. The Brook daughter takes one look at her sister and lets out a blood-curdling scream. Then she turns and runs, yelping every time her bare feet hit the rocky ground. The other Brooks look at Lily in shock, as do the guards—now huddled together, shaking and shivering with fright—and the Lily Brook residents.

"But you're dead!" The rotten-toothed brother gapes at his sister.

"Oh, no." Lily shakes her head, her brown hair glowing in the light from the bonfire. "I'm not dead at all."

"But the volcano." The Brook brother with the long, knotted hair peers doubtfully at her. "You fell right inside. There wasn't a trace of you left."

"Oh, that. I landed right onto Dr. Caruthers, world-renowned scientist and volcano explorer. "

"You *what*?" Mrs. Brook's eyes are bulging from her pudgy face.

"Neither of us was injured by the fall," Lily assures her. "Nothing but goose eggs and bruises. But it was all in the name of science, as Dr. Caruthers says. When I fell, I dislodged a fossil, a rather unique specimen that has since been named the *Lilisaurus*."

"The Lily-Saurus?" Mr. Brook, whose withered body is covered with a ragged, mud-stained toga, appeared to have been shocked into silence by the transformations going on around him, but now he spits out his daughter's name as if just the sound of it makes him quite ill.

"It was my first of many discoveries. Dr. Caruthers says my klutziness is my greatest asset—I am always tripping over new discoveries and stumbling into new ideas. He agreed to be my mentor, and I changed my name to Lily Caruthers, to celebrate my new life as a scientist."

"Caruthers, Caruthers," Mrs. Brook is muttering to herself. "I've heard that name before."

"Dr. Caruthers is quite famous. It's possible you've read about him. Or perhaps you've heard a thing or two about me. I once wrote an article about that very mountain." She turns and points towards Mount Poplova. "I discussed the myth of the wishing well that some Poplovastanis believe is located in a cave at its base."

"Argh!" Mrs. Brook turns away from Lily and limp-runs across the rocky ground towards the horizon. Her raggedy dress and her scraggly hair billow out behind her.

The Brook brothers each let out a similar cry and go charging after their mother. The sour scent of them is carried back in the wind until they are tiny specks on the horizon.

"I don't see why everyone is so upset." Lily turns to her father. "I've forgiven you for that incident in the air balloon. In fact, I'm thankful that you pushed me out. If you hadn't, I would never have met Dr. Caruthers, I would never have become a famous scientist, and I would never have …" But Mr. Brook is no longer listening. He has started to run after his sons.

"You've forgiven us?" he screams over his shoulder, when he is a few yards away. "*You've* forgiven *us*? It was you who ruined *our* lives, Lily."

"They needn't have left in such a hurry," Lily murmurs, the entire Brook family now out of sight. "I was going to say that I'm terribly rich and that I could have helped them. I had no idea they were living in such utter poverty." She turns then and looks at us all, close to five hundred people in black pants and blazers with her initials embroidered over the pocket, a handful of guards in their stiff gray uniforms, not including Captain Ma'am, with her braid unraveling, a frizz of tangled orange hair framing her sour-looking face. And in the center of it all the King of Poplovastan, who has picked up the can of well water and is beaming into it.

"Who *are* you people?"

EMILY TAKES A STEP towards Lily. "We're from Lily Brook." Lily looks shocked to hear Emily use her name, but Emily continues. She tells Lily about the Lily Brook Academy brochure, and about how we have all been sent here because we are ordinary. She tells her how day in and day out we've all slaved at cutting down Poplova Forest, and how five of us made it to the well at the mountain's base and brought back a can of water. The King has the rusty can resting on his lap, and Emily gestures to it.

Everyone is silent while Emily speaks to Lily. Every time she pauses, though, the King opens his mouth to add something. But Emily is so intent on recounting our adventure that she doesn't notice. Finally, the King can't contain himself any longer.

"But who went with you, child?" he demands. "That's the most important detail."

"Maggie, Trevor, and Uncle Ernst." Emily points to them as she says their names, and the King stares hard. "And Danny."

When the King looks at me, I smile.

"Aha," he says, nodding vigorously. "I thought as much." He leans back in his chair, beaming, and motions for Emily to continue.

When Emily has told the story through, ending at the part when the Brooks have become paupers and Lily Brook herself arrives, Lily approaches the King.

"Is there any water left?"

"A small amount," he says.

She leans over him to stare into the tin can. "So this is it?" She holds it to her nose and sniffs. She dips her finger in and swirls it around. She swishes it, and then, "Oops." The can slips from her hand and lands on the rocks at her feet. The water splashes onto the dirt, all except for one cold drop, and that drop lands on the corner of my lip. Without thinking, I stick out my tongue and lick it off.

AS SOON AS I LICK THAT DROP, I realize my mistake. I start to feel dizzy.

"He's glowing!" someone shouts. I glance down at my arms, and sure enough they seem to be radiating light. Terrified, I squeeze my eyes shut. All I can think of is the cave picture that showed flames leaping from the head of the person with the blank face. Will I catch fire? Is this the great fear of mine that is about to come true? Or are there even worse things in store? Will Captain Ma'am take me out to the pit behind the guardhouse and make me bathe with maggots? Will the Brooks come back and lock me up in Lily Brook forever? I am imagining the horrors that await me when I hear a familiar voice, a most beautiful voice, call my name.

"Danny! Oh, my dearest Danny Boy!"

When I open my eyes to the sight of Mother running towards me, at first I'm afraid I'm hallucinating—Uncle Ernst did say that the stagnant well water could be poisonous. But I can't be, because everyone else seems to see Mother too. A tight circle forms around us, and some of the Lily Brook residents reach out their fingers to touch her arms, her hair, perhaps to see if she's real. "Who are you? Where did you come from?" they ask, but Mother doesn't answer. She's just gripping me tightly against her, repeating, "Why it *can't* be. But it *is*. But it *can't* be."

"So it is," cries the King. He has changed into the clothes that landed on his lap when the trunks exploded: a crisp white shirt, a red bow tie, and a purple velvet suit. He places a hand on Mother's shoulder, and when she turns to him her mouth drops open.

"My dear, dear girl, how much I have missed you." He pulls Mother into a hug. How much he'd missed her? How would he have even met her? What could he possibly mean by that? But then Mother pulls away and strokes her fingers across the top button of the King's suit jacket—a small gold button with an image of a crown stamped in the center.

"I knew the first time I set eyes on the boy," the King says. "I just knew he must have been a child of yours."

Mother keeps stroking the King's jacket, but she doesn't respond. She's staring over his shoulder—at the piles of strewn clothes and toys, at the metal and other debris glinting in the firelight, at the hundreds of old and ragged-looking Lily Brook residents and the handful of fierce guards.

"What is this place, Danny?" she whispers. "What are you doing here?"

The other Lily Brook residents crowd more tightly around Mother and me as I tell her about Lily Brook. They interrupt to add details—about the rickety bunks, the cruel treatment, the days spent chopping wild trees. Trevor tells Mother about some of the worst supper soup combinations, and Uncle Ernst whispers about his time spent in the dungeon when he first arrived. When Mother starts to sob, Maggie strokes her arm. "It's okay," she whispers. "You didn't know."

"Oh, Danny Boy, I'm so very sorry," Mother cries. "How awful it sounds. Why didn't you mention it in your letters?" She pulls a stack of white envelopes from her pocket, all addressed to Mother in the same awkward loops of my usual handwriting. "The horseback-riding, the swimming, the helicopter trips. You seemed to be having so much fun!"

From beside the bonfire someone starts laughing. "How about the go-karts?" Captain Ma'am sneers. "I'm sure we mentioned them too. And the dozens and dozens of kind teachers and wonderful friends."

Captain Ma'am's words are all it takes for us to be reminded of the guards still among us, most of whom are tucked inside the shadows, attempting invisibility. With Emily in the lead, a group of Lily Brookers march over to surround them. Failing miserably at appearing fierce, the Lily Brookers crack their knuckles and flex their arms, Some of the men twist their mustaches into sharp points.

"Who is that dreadful woman?" Mother asks, trying to peer at Captain Ma'am through the crowd.

"She's the worst of the guards," Trevor says. "She's a complete terror." And even Maggie, who I've never heard say a cruel word about anyone, nods in agreement.

I climb onto a boulder to see through the wall of Lily Brookers. In the light from the bonfire, Mother Ma'am looks as pale as the moon. She tucks herself between Bob and Captain Ma'am and bends down so she's barely visible over their heads.

"What should we do about them?" demands Emily. But before anyone has a chance to answer, there's a great roar overhead and gusts of wind blow through the thread-bare sleeves of our Lily Brook blazers.

WHEN MR. REMRODDINGER steps from his plane, he's on his cell phone and doesn't even look up at us. The airplane continues down the rocky ground and lifts again into the sky as Mr. Remroddinger walks across the gravel that used to be a golden path and reaches for the place where only minutes earlier there had been a door handle. He twists his hand back and forth in the air and then switches off his phone and lifts his head, puzzled. His mouth drops open at the rubble that has replaced the Brooks' castle, and drops further when he sees the lot of us: five hundred Lily Brook residents surrounding the shaking, shivering guards, the King sitting tall in his glorious purple suit, and Lily Brook herself standing in the shadows, watching everything play out with great interest.

"It's that awful little man," Mother gasps. She drops my hand and begins to march over, but before she reaches Mr. Remroddinger, the circle of angry Lily Brook residents expands to envelop him.

"We could tie them up and leave them here," one Lily Brooker suggests.

"Dump them in the forest."

"Feed them to wild beasts."

"Make them do our bidding like trained monkeys."

The suggestions are endless. Then: "Let's just let them go." Uncle Ernst steps back from the circle. "I for one would prefer never to lay eyes on them again." A few others nod their heads and mumble in agreement.

"Fine." A stocky No-Wit girl with bushy eyebrows and a thick blond braid waves a group of residents back, creating an escape route for the quivering guards. "You've got ten seconds to vamoose, but if you don't," she sneers, in a voice frighteningly similar to Captain Ma'am's, "there's no telling what's in store for you." She starts to count, and the guards scatter in every direction. By the time she reaches "five" none of them are in sight, but at "one" most of them have started to slink back again. Mother Ma'am leads the group of returning guards. She's sobbing, and when she's within earshot again she cries out, in a voice much louder than I would have imagined her capable of, "Please, don't make us leave. We're just as much victims of circumstance as you folks are."

"See, she *is* sad," Maggie whispers to me. "She probably only acts mean because she's unhappy."

But the rest of the Lily Brookers aren't as forgiving as Maggie. "We are not victims of circumstance," one of the young Lily Brookers reminds Mother Ma'am. "We're victims of you lot." He takes a step towards her, and Mother Ma'am grabs Mr. Remroddinger and thrusts him in front of her as a shield.

"But it's *his* fault. He *made* me do it."

Mr. Remroddinger tries to escape Mother Ma'am's grip, but she's holding on tight.

"Ten years ago my father lost our family's fortune at the horse races," she sobs. "We were living in a rented apartment, and I was actually *working* in a *Laundromat* to make ends meet. Then he came in one day." She thrusts Mr. Remroddinger forward a step. "He'd read about my family's misfortune and offered me a job at Lily Brook. And I had no other choice. At the laundry they put me in charge of delicates. Delicates!" she repeats in a wail. "I had to wash dirty underwear with my bare hands!"

In a low voice that reminds me of Mother Ma'am's, Trevor hisses, "Whine, whine, whine."

"I expect it *was* quite upsetting for her," Maggie says.

Mother, who has left the edge of the circle of Lily Brookers and is now clutching my hand, doesn't say anything. She just squeezes harder.

One by one the guards tell their sob stories; they all came from wealthy families who lost everything. Bob fidgets and looks quite uncomfortable. In a whisper, he tells us that Mr. Remroddinger had come upon him in a science lab. After his father went bankrupt, Bob had agreed to be experimented on in exchange for enough money to pay the mortgage on his family's villa.

"I couldn't continue," he whimpers. "I spent each and every day with wires poking out of me. My nose hair started falling out in clumps. Everything I ate tasted like raw chicken." Trevor starts to laugh as Bob thrusts his right foot towards us. "And I had to learn to walk all over again after they shrunk my feet!"

Maggie gasps in shock, but Trevor's giggling is infectious, and I let out a snort of laughter as well.

"I'd like to hear from that awful woman with the braid," Mother whispers. She's not alone. Most of the Lily Brookers have turned towards Captain Ma'am. The shadows the moonlight casts across her face make her look fiercer than ever.

"What?" She barks. "You expect a sad little story from me as well? Well, you're not getting one." She crosses her arms over her chest and glares at us.

But Mr. Remroddinger seems unable to hold back. "It was I who thought to write a letter blaming Lily for her own death," he brags. "It was I who thought to hide it in her locket, and it was I who organized the search party that discovered it. I suggested the Brooks kidnap the

King in order to take ownership of Poplova Forest, and I went around to your snooty families and secured full registration year after year. I searched out the guards and brought them to Lily Brook." He is shaking his head, quite proud of himself. "But Elmira," he points at Captain Ma'am, "she was by far my greatest contribution to the Lily Brook empire.

"Elmira was twenty-two when I found her, the year before Lily Brook opened. Her parents had gone to jail for embezzlement and she was living alone in a dingy basement apartment, awaiting trial for a series of garbage truck hijackings. She'd emptied the trucks on the lawns of former friends who had failed to rescue her from poverty. I bailed her out immediately and rushed her to the Brooks. I just knew she would make you little twerps tremble in your stockings." He gazes at Captain Ma'am with admiration.

"I was sure she couldn't have been from around here," Mother says. "If there's one thing I remember from my childhood, it's how kind everyone was."

"You're from Poplovastan?" Trevor turns to stare at Mother. He looks appalled, as if he couldn't imagine anything worse.

"I suppose I am," Mother says. "For the longest time, I didn't remember. But I think I grew up in a little cottage at the edge of that forest."

"Is that how you know the King?" Maggie's question is for Mother, but when I glance at her she's staring at me, the edges of her lips turned up in a slight smile.

Mother begins to tell my friends about her childhood: about the tree that fell on her parent's cabin and the couple who adopted her from the orphanage. It's the first time I've heard her tell the story all at once, but even though I want to know more, I can't concentrate on what she's saying. There's a faint fizzling coming from the direction of the forest. In the moonlight I see sparks shooting from the top of Mount Poplova.

"Look!" I point towards the mountain. There are screams and wails, and many of the Lily Brookers begin to scatter in every direction. Others pile up their suitcases and stand on top of them to get a better view.

"How thrilling!" Lily shouts, clapping her hands.

An explosion sounds, and though it is difficult to see the mountain in the moonlight, it seems that something is spraying into the air from its peak. The trees begin to rustle and shake, and then the ones lining the edge of the forest lean apart. Through them blasts a giant flood of water. A great wave rushes at us, with a pile of debris on its crest, and then retreats just inches before it touches our feet—hurtling the wreckage towards us.

Except it isn't debris.

It isn't wreckage.

It is almost one hundred soggy and coughing ex-Lily Brookers.

José lands on the jacket Emily is still clutching, knocking them both to the ground. He sits up and shakes the water out of his ears, then looks around him.

"What happened?" he asks, as a small gold button falls from his shirtsleeve and rolls to a stop against my shoe.

EPILOGUE
One Year Later

"THIS SOUP IS PROBABLY THE BEST YET." With my fingers, I scrape the last drops from the bottom of the can. "What's in it?"

Maggie shrugs. "You know Trevor and Louisa are always experimenting." She places my empty can on the lunch tray beside hers and heads for the kitchen.

I follow. We were late for lunch and, except for a group of women in lab coats examining rock specimens on a shelf by the entrance, the mess hall is empty. The tables have been wiped clean and the chairs are stacked by the far wall under the menu board, where "Supper Soup" is scrawled beneath "Lunch."

Even before we reach the kitchen door we hear yowling coming from the other side.

"Drop it!" I shout when I enter. Archduke Pooch has a purple spatula sticking from his mouth. The handle—which Emily is tugging at—is covered in slobber and tooth marks. Emily and Pooch both let go at once.

"We're just playing." Emily's frizzy hair is pulled into her signature pigtails. "Go on, Pooch, it's okay. Besides," she says, pointing to a wooden crate on the counter, "there's plenty where that one came from. Uncle Ernst sent us about a hundred spatulas yesterday. He even had one designed specially for scraping out soup tins."

"And it works great." Trevor's at his usual spot next to the stove, a row of nine cans lined up on the counter in front of him. He's got a tenth can tipped to his mouth and is using a small spade-shaped spatula to scrape out the last drops of soup. Housed in the open cupboard behind him is his spice collection. It has grown considerably over the past year, as many of the visiting scientists bring gifts of spices from their home countries.

Louisa, Emily's family's former cook and Lily Brook's greatest new asset, is at the counter chopping mangoes. She scoops the slices off the cutting board and into two bowls of fruit salad on the counter. "Dessert, kids?"

"No thanks, Louisa; I should get back." I pat my leg, and Pooch picks up the spatula in his mouth and follows me out the back door.

IN THE YEAR SINCE the Brooks left Lily Brook, the compound has changed quite a bit: the six bunkers have been replaced by a cluster of cottages, the fence torn down, and laboratories built beside the ruins of the Royals' castle. The mess hall, however, has been left pretty much as it was. Apparently, some of the scholars who come to the Lily Brook Institute for the Study of Mount Poplova enjoy learning first-hand about the history of the place. Soup served in tin cans, dungeon tours, piles of machetes at the edge of the forest, and glimpses of some of Lily Brook's ex-guards are all part of the experience.

Sometimes I feel sorry for the Lily Brookers who still live at the Institute. The day Lily Brook was liberated, Mr. Remroddinger's cell phone was commandeered for hours. Call after call was made, flights were booked, and homecomings were organized. But not for everyone. My friends were among the group who didn't have a home to return to. Trevor, Maggie, and José all dialed their families to find the numbers had been disconnected, and Emily's father asked her to repeat her name three times before hanging up on her. Luckily, Louisa was eavesdropping on the other line.

For the first time in Lily Brook's history, however, no one seems to mind living here. In fact, some Lily Brookers who left to be reunited with their families returned to Lily Brook as soon as the Institute opened. The words of the Brooks' brochure are finally coming true: Lily Brook residents have actually chosen to make a life for themselves here. And Emily has welcomed them all.

IF ANYONE TELLS YOU that a thirteen-year-old isn't capable of running a research institute, you can be sure they haven't met Emily Buckler. Emily takes care of everything at Lily Brook. She keeps track of all the visiting scientists, providing them with detailed itineraries for their stays, and she stays on top of all maintenance issues—a light bulb won't be burned out for more than five minutes before Emily has dispatched a work crew to replace it.

The work crews—made up of Lily Brook's paid employees, the former guards—are Emily's greatest brainchild. The visiting scientists always mention how impressed they are by the crews that take care of every-thing from gardening to construction. *So efficient,* they say. *And so pleasant, too.*

Maggie spends her days working for Healing House, one of Lily Brook's most famous laboratories. The scientists at Healing House create medicine derived from plant species found in Poplova Forest. Maggie probably does the most of anyone at Healing House, though. She's always bringing back roots and leaves from her walks in the woods—and they often prove to be perfect cures for coughs and colds, or for headaches and fevers.

She even created a concoction of bark and flower petals that helped Bob's hands and feet return to nearly their normal size.

While Maggie is curing diseases and Emily is keeping things in order, I'm usually wandering around the forest with Pooch, drawing maps of everything I find; I'm in charge of marking where trails should be built and where rock piles need to be cleared. Poplova Forest is much different now. The tree bark is as soft as velvet, the vines hang loosely from branches, and the once-translucent bugs are brightly colored, some with striped or dappled wings. Even the birds and animals have returned to their forest home.

<hr />

UP AHEAD OF ME NOW, a crew of former Lily Brook guards is snipping the overgrown vines from the path with silver scissors. I can hear whistling even before I see the troop of men and women in black pants, white shirts, and black blazers.

"Hello, Danny," they call as I pass. Or at least most of them do. Captain Ma'am, who people now call by her first name, hasn't quite warmed up to the idea of being friendly. She glares at me, and angles her scissors in a threatening point.

"I saw that, Elmira!" José, who's in charge of the work crews, comes rushing down the path. José's a lot more pleasant now that Emily had a dance studio built at the edge of the forest, but he's still as tough as ever. Emily decided that of all the ex-residents, he was the one best suited to keep a special eye on Captain Ma'am.

"Now, what," he asks her, "is the Lily Brook motto?"

Captain Ma'am only glowers at him.

"Can anyone help Elmira out?"

Bob raises his hand. "At Lily Brook, kindness is everything."

After a long pause, Captian Ma'am sneers at me. "Pleasure to see you, Danny."

José nods, then claps his hands, setting the guards back to work before he lounges beside them on a fallen log.

Clearing the paths isn't the difficult job it was when it was up to the Lily Brook residents. The vines don't grow back as soon as they're cut, the twigs don't stab, and the branches don't thwack you off balance when you get too close. In fact, Poplova Forest is the same as any other forest.

Almost.

I start to walk away and a vine curls around my arm, pulling me sideways. I turn, and as I do the vine uncurls and then twists to form an arrow that points towards Captain Ma'am. Suddenly, it smacks her across the back of her head.

A couple guards rush to see if she's okay (kindness is everything at Lily Brook), but José has fallen to the ground in hysterics. He may be the guards' supervisor, but whenever they're on trail duty he can usually count on the trees to take care of things for him.

⸺⸰⸰⸰⸺

BECAUSE THE KING'S CASTLE was destroyed when the Brooks drank the well water, he had a new one built at the far edge of the forest. That's where Archduke Pooch and I are heading. Home. As soon as it comes into view, Pooch bounds ahead up the stairs.

My sisters were more than willing to move to Poplovastan. Annabelle has finally found something she considers more beautiful than herself, and now spends her days filling her sketchpad with drawings of Mount Poplova. Caroline uses the mountain and the forest surrounding it as her specialized training facility. As for Brittany, Lily Brook has become her mentor, and all of Poplovastan is her laboratory. Father, however, wasn't exactly keen on the relocation idea. Until the King offered to let him help run the country. As I walk past, I glance through the doorway of his office.

Father is lying on a leather couch in front of the fireplace, an eye-mask over his eyes, faintly snoring. His single advisor, Mr. Remroddinger, is on a chair beside him in his black monogrammed blazer, performing the only tasks he ever seems to do these days—he's reading aloud from the *Financial Times* and massaging Father's feet.

I run up the marble staircase two by two and head into the front room. Pooch has already curled up on the velvet couch between Mother and the King.

"Danny Boy." Mother holds out her arms to hug me. "We were hoping you'd be back soon. Look what the King found today."

From the other side of the couch, the King beams and hands me a photograph.

I recognize the two people immediately. The man has curly hair and unruly eyebrows. He's dressed in a striped shirt, faded blue trousers, and boots that reach almost to his knees. Beside him, clutching his hand, is a small girl wearing an ankle-length, fur-collared coat.

The photograph looks ancient, but it can't be. I saw this man and his daughter only a year ago. They were the ones who walked out of Poplova Forest, past Emily, Maggie, Trevor, and me. They were the ones who made me decide to risk going in myself.

"Who are they?"

"Don't you recognize the coat, Danny?" Mother points to the girl. "That's your great-grandmother with your great-great-grandfather, Zuther."

And it's true. The girl is wearing Mother's coat. It's not as ratty as it is now. The elbows aren't worn and the hem isn't frayed, but it's definitely the same one.

"You may keep it, Danny," the King says, when I start to leave the room, still clutching the photograph.

I mumble a thank-you from my bedroom doorway, then close the door behind me and prop the photo on my windowsill, where I have a clear view of Mount Poplova. I can even see the rocks that fell from the mountain during the eruption and which now cover the entrance of the cave. The cave where my great-great-grandfather, Zuther, dug his daughter a well. The well that was the reason Lily Brook was built, and the reason it was destroyed. It's the only rock pile I've instructed the work crews not to remove.

Acknowledgments

BUILDING A BOOK from a pile of words is a little like searching for a wishing well in the middle of a dangerous forest—it's impossible without help. Thank you to everyone who lent a hand during the journey.

For ensuring I was well equipped: the McTrunkverts—Mum, Richard, and James.

For pointing me in the right direction, my first readers: Margery (Gran) McKay, Katie Brownhill, and Kathi Pollard.

For clearing the path: Jennifer Caloyeras, Sue Fast, David Poulsen, and our fearless leader, Glen Huser.

For slipping me through the cave's entrance: Zsuzsi Gartner.

For welcoming me in: the Annick team.

For examining my rope, and fixing the slipped knots: Pam Robertson and Tanya Trafford.

And for being there every step along the way, scavenging for food, fending off danger, and holding my hand during the darkest moments: Mike McLean.

About the Author

LAURA TRUNKEY lives in Victoria, British Columbia, where she works at a school that is nothing like Lily Brook. *The Incredibly Ordinary Danny Chandelier* is her first novel.